OFF THE RESERVATION

A Novel

Glen Merzer

vividthoughts

Published by Vivid Thoughts Press, Atlanta, Georgia
www.vividthoughtspress.com

ISBN: 0692315160
ISBN 13: 9780692315163
Library of Congress Control Number: 2014913020
Vivid Thoughts Press, Atlanta, GA
Printed in the U.S.A.

For Joanna

I realized now that after having successfully passed the trial of the nocturnal terrors, of the tempest, I had to submit to the acid test: the temptation to return.—Alejo Carpentier, *The Lost Steps*

OFF THE RESERVATION

CHAPTER ONE

The Decision

*C*ongressman Evan Gorgoni trimmed his mustache, snipping along a millimeter above his upper lip, up the left side and down the right—for he was a lefty—with his trusty little green-handled hair scissors that his mother had given him as a coming-of-age present when he set off some thirty-five years ago from Lebanon, Indiana, for Bloomington. The mustache had become an almost permanent fixture on his face ever since his junior year at Indiana University, when his first serious girlfriend, and the only to render his manhood a form of leash, suggested it.

He had once shaved the mustache off and kept it off for several weeks, a few years back, after that plane landed on the Hudson. Too many of his friends in Washington had begun to comment on his resemblance to the newly famous and similarly mustached Captain "Sully" Sullenberger—even a Washington Post scribe couldn't resist the allusion. As the embarrassment he felt at being compared, if only superficially, to a genuine American hero was a bit much for him to take, he resorted to his razor. Besides, the comparison grated on him, as he was more than a decade younger than Sully, and surely he looked younger with his fuller head of hair. The hair was not nearly as thick as it once was, though, and it was every bit as grey-white as Sully's. He had developed his own marker of aging: people no longer called him *prematurely* grey. In fact, they had stopped describing him that way at about forty. By now, after all, at fifty-three, he had attained the age at which it was pretty hard to be prematurely anything. *Sans* the mustache, though, he hadn't felt quite himself. Everyone had told him to grow it back, and so, like a well-trained politician, he did.

He stepped out of the bathroom and into the bedroom, where Caroline stood in her nightgown leaning over the bed, fluffing the pillows, as she had done every night of the twenty-one years of their marriage. It still amused him. What exactly was the point of fluffing pillows that their heads would unceremoniously un-fluff in a few minutes' time? He had asked that question of Caroline many years ago, before she became his wife, and she had given him that look of relationship-seriousness, that look in equal parts assertive and vulnerable, that single women come to generate as they pass thirty. *I can't sleep on a pillow that is not fluffed,* she had said. *You should know that about me right now.* Occasionally, in his apartment in Washington, D.C. that he shared with Congressman Jake Busby, he would remember to fluff his pillow in her honor. Occasionally.

"The energy bill's dead," he said. "The Leader said she'd try to bring it back next session in a scaled-down form."

"Better than nothing," Caroline said. She was wearing her brown hair short these days, a reality to which he was still adjusting. She had used the term *pageboy*, though he wasn't too clear on what that meant. Her frame was as trim as it was on the day they met, twenty-two years ago, when the school board hired her to defend it against the only person he could remember ever hating him, an embittered and litigious ex-teacher of English, for whom reading was not as important as expression, and expression could take the form of body piercing. He had told the teacher, whose classes were by most measures out of control, that she was nuts. It was not quite as diplomatic as the language he usually employed as principal, though it had seemed more than apt at the time.

He gazed at his wife with the admiration he always felt for her tenacity, her steadiness, her sense of command; the pillows were getting the brunt of it now. She smiled at him, as she still occasionally did for no reason at all, as if they were young lovers. Her skin seemed all but impervious to wrinkles, though a few had made inroads near her eyes, especially when she laughed. She was never a big laugher but that made her all the more lovely when mirth overtook her.

"It'll have to be good enough for the glaciers," he said. He swallowed two capsules of cayenne and washed them down with the bottle of spring water he kept by the bed.

"How much did your new consultant say we'd need?"

"One point two. By next spring."

"That's doable. We've already got three hundred grand in the till."

"I've got nothing to run on. Haven't gotten a bill passed in—"

She finished with the fluffing.

"Evan, people want to vote for the small-town boy who put himself through school driving a rig, became an educator, a principal, a community leader—that's what they care about. The man, not any dumb piece of legislation."

"I was under the impression that I was supposed to be a legislator. I didn't realize my job was just to be a man."

He lay down and pulled the sheet over him. In an instant, she threw the sheet right off and threw herself where the sheet had been. She kissed him in the wet way she kissed when she meant business.

"It is *now*," she said.

He looked at her with surprise.

"Good thing I took that cayenne," he said.

⟨————⟩

You could still see the outline of the old baseball diamond on the soccer field, the new grass not yet fully camouflaging it, the old home plate area visible near the goalposts that Nicole and her teammates in yellow could not have succeeded in avoiding more adeptly had that been their perverse intent. Gorgoni sat between Caroline and their sixteen-year-old daughter Mandy, who manifested her exasperation as she watched the yellow Jackson Creek Middle School Jaguars get shellacked. "Get the ball, Nicole!" she cried in vain, groaning when a tall girl in an orange jersey kicked the soccer ball well over her sister's head, as Nicole ducked pointlessly. Mandy had the gift of appearing to care about matters like sports that concerned her not at all; she had already discovered that life was more fun that way. She had red hair and freckles and at five-foot-nine—a mere inch shy of her father's height—the longest legs in the extended family.

Gorgoni looked away from the field. A homeless man was pushing a squeaky shopping cart full of possessions along the park path between the soccer field and the tennis courts, his shambling gait exacerbated by erratic arm gestures. Gorgoni stared blankly at the pathetic spectacle. All day, he had felt strangely unnerved, beaten up, numb; he had been shocked by how pale and drawn he looked in the mirror in the morning. *Angst* was new to him; he couldn't explain it and he refused to embrace it. He had a life about which he could not make a complaint. A wife he loved. Two daughters he adored. A relatively safe seat in Congress. More friends than he could count. The esteem of his community. And yet he was drowning in an exhausting, exasperating sea of futility.

The June sun beat on him. He could use some color on his skin, but he wished he had worn a baseball cap. His skull was burning up, despite his damp hair. Caroline had nearly emptied the single small plastic bottle of water they brought; he took a sip.

Mandy turned to him with a gripe. "She's playing like…" She looked at him strangely. "What's wrong, Dad?"

A tear had apparently made its way down his cheek. He wiped it away before Caroline could turn her head in his direction.

"Nothing." The orange team scored a goal, and the homeless guy cheered as if he'd won a high-stakes bet. "Hey, should I cook tonight?" Gorgoni said. "How about I make my classic shiitake stew?"

"Now *I'm* going to cry," Mandy said.

When the game finally ended, and the teams shook hands and parted ways, Mandy was the first to hug a dejected and sweaty Nicole, her chin resting atop Nicole's cap, as her parents stood alongside.

"You displayed superb sportsmanship," Mandy said, cheerfully.

"Give me a break," Nicole said. She was a skinny, awkward, undeveloped twelve-year-old with dark eyebrows and green eyes that would clearly be alluring one day; they were waiting for her body to catch up. "We got creamed. Four zip."

"The team played well, though," Caroline said.

Nicole gave her father a guilty look. "I can't believe you flew home to witness this travesty, Dad. Didn't you have anything important to vote on?"

"No. Once I voted to table the motion to reconsider the vote to adopt the conference committee report as previously amended, my job was done and nothing could keep me from this humiliation."

They headed towards the parking lot in the stifling heat. Gorgoni mopped his forehead with a handkerchief. He stopped to rub his eyes; salty sweat had invaded them. Caroline, Mandy, and Nicole continued on for several paces without noticing that he had failed to keep up. He looked up at the punishing sun, an orange orb blazing in a cloudless sky.

Was that a rock under his spine? Why—why the hell was he on his back? And why did it hurt? And whose voice had that been—that child's voice? There was still salt in his eyes. "We need an ambulance immediately!" Mandy was saying, somewhere nearby, her voice echoing as if in a tunnel. "It's for Congressman Evan Gorgoni." The air shimmered, and through it he saw the foggy form of his wife leaning down over him to gently slap his face. All her edges had gone soft to the point of disappearing; she looked like a human cloud.

"Evan? Evan?"

"Hmmm?"

"What happened?"

"What do you mean? I'm fine."

"You collapsed. Mandy called 911."

"Oh, no. What for?"

"Because you collapsed. Do you feel chest pain?"

"No."

He sat up. Mandy gave him her water bottle; he took a swig.

"Oh, Dad, you scared us," she said.

"I'm sorry. But I don't need medics—"

"You were totally out," Nicole said. "For like a minute."

"More like twenty seconds," Mandy said.

"No, more like a minute," Nicole said.

"It was less than that."

"Next time we'll time it."

"I'm fine," Gorgoni said. "We'll send the ambulance back."

"No, you're going to get checked out," Caroline said.

"I really don't want to," Gorgoni said. He reached for a hand up.

"Honey, you don't get a vote on this one," Caroline said. "Maybe you should just sit there a while longer."

"Not once," Caroline said, definitively, perched on the edge of the bed, plucking a card from the tray table and reading it. Monroe Hospital called them Cheer Cards; he already had dozens of them around the room, though he'd suffered less than forty-eight hours in its anodyne environs. The Leader had sent flowers, Jake Busby called him twice with concern, and April Madrue, his scarily efficient, obese Chief of Staff, had phoned frequently with more cheer than a card could contain. Several of the nurses had assured him that he had their vote, though no election was near, and the doctors couldn't have been friendlier. All the same, the food was piss-poor, and the place smelled vaguely of bleach. It depressed him to spend whole days in an oddly defective nightgown, and he wanted nothing more than to flee the joint.

"Never?" he said, scratching his nose. "Not even after some rubber chicken fundraising dinner?"

"We always eat before we get there. Screw their food."

"You never wanted me to get out of the game?"

"No."

"Will you blame me if I do?"

Caroline looked up from the Cheer Card. She studied him for a long moment, then once again gave the card her attention, or appeared to.

"Of course not."

"That took a long time for *of course not.*"

"I wouldn't blame you, but I'd be disappointed."

"Even after—?"

"They ran every test on you imaginable. You're fine. Must have been dehydration."

"The doctor said that wasn't likely."

"The doctor has no clue."

He smiled. Caroline had enormous faith in medical care in the abstract and little confidence in any physician in particular.

"It was your idea that I run for the State House and then Congress. Now and again you float a shot at the Senate. I've been your vessel for the last twenty years."

"That's not fair."

"Caroline, you're the Ivy-educated Brahmin lawyer. I'm just a regular working-class Hoosier. Why didn't you run for office?"

"I believe you just answered your own question."

"You could have faked the common touch. The Kennedys made an art of it."

"People warm to you more than—I'm not the one they want to have a beer with. So let them vote for you, and I get to whisper in your ear about fair labor practices and—"

He looked out the window. He had a view of a lush green lawn and an old sycamore. Two squirrels were chasing each other in a spiral up the trunk of the sycamore. They ran in spurts, then stopped in sync, then resumed their upward spiral again.

"I'm losing touch with...You know what Mandy said when she called 911? *We need an ambulance for Congressman Evan Gorgoni.* She didn't say *for my father.*"

Caroline shrugged dismissively. "Well, she probably thought they'd show up faster for a congressman."

"Uh-huh."

She squinted at him. "How'd you hear what she said if you were passed out?"

Now it was his turn to shrug, unconcerned. Caroline sat straight-backed, clear-eyed, the picture of health. She tilted her head and looked at him as if considering that he might require further medical evaluation. He took a deep breath and screwed up his courage. "I can't do it anymore, Caroline. I'm not going to run again."

She wore now the enigmatic expression that she had worn a year earlier when he had rather decisively, he thought, rejected her suggestion of a ten-day vacation in Spain. It was an expression that was hard to read but bespoke some mysterious power she possessed over him, perhaps not entirely unrelated to the sway of his first serious girlfriend. In the end, truth be told, he had found the Basque countryside mesmerizing, the architecture of Barcelona delightful, and he would never forget that museum in Bilbao.

"You don't have to decide now. Get some rest and—"

"No, I've decided, and I have to be fair to the party; they've got to find someone else. Something happened to me while I was out. I don't want to call it a vision. I wouldn't want to minimize the thing."

"Uh-huh." Caroline nodded in the way she did when she was not persuaded.

"It came to me in something like a dream but I was—somehow I was hyper-aware. I could feel the blood coursing through my veins. And I heard something like—like a command."

"You heard a command?"

"In a child's voice. But with authority. With certainty. Telling me to go for the thing that sings."

"Go for the thing that sings?"

"I don't know what the hell it means."

"That's odd."

"Yeah." He rubbed his chin a few times between his thumb and forefinger. "But I'm going to try."

Nicole appeared to enjoy wheeling her father out of the hospital. She sped with him through the lobby, jostling the leaves of a potted fern.

"Don't run anyone over," Caroline said.

"That would be a cool headline," Nicole said. "Congressman bulldozes pedestrian in hospital."

"God, they poked me a lot," Gorgoni said. "They ran every test on me except IQ."

"I'm sure that would have come up negative, too," Mandy said, to her sister's amusement.

"What are you laughing at?" Gorgoni said.

"She's my role model," Nicole said.

"You're making a mistake," Gorgoni said.

Outside the door, Gorgoni bolted upright and exhaled like a man released from prison. No better tonic for the soul, he reflected, than escape from the world of health care. He would relax at home. It was a goal that seemed almost unattainable, unimaginable, but there it was. He would relax.

Odd, how he remembered the feel of the mallet in his hand. He hadn't set eyes on the croquet set in over a decade. He set up the course strategically, placing the wickets far apart to make the play challenging in the sloping, rectangular backyard. He had only the dimmest recollection of the rules, but it hardly mattered since he was playing by himself. He set the beaten-up blue ball in the center of the yard, chose a direction to aim, and gave it a satisfying thwack. The ball rolled towards the hedges. Three more strokes and he was positioned to finally traverse a wicket, when Caroline approached, looking especially summery in white Capris, an embroidered white blouse and oval sunglasses with a blue tint.

"Evan, I didn't know we still had this set. I haven't seen it since Mandy was a child. Where'd you find it?"

"Basement."

"What were you doing there?"

"Looking for the croquet set. You know, this is actually a much better game than golf. It takes more skill to get a big ball through a hoop than a little one into a hole. Golfers make a big deal about distance but that's just so they can ride in that cart. Let the Republicans have golf. Croquet is for the working people. Whether they know it or not."

She raised her sunglasses to her forehead. "Want me to play with you?"

It was not a question for which he was prepared. It had him flummoxed a little bit. He hadn't felt this way since the lamentable

Sunday on *Face the Nation* when he was asked his position on the proper response to China's devaluation of the yuan. Even April Madrue hadn't seen that one coming. On the yuan issue, he had vamped and equivocated, but that strategy wouldn't fly now with his croquet dilemma. His wife could be more deadly with the follow-ups than Bob Schieffer. He scratched his head, rubbed his eyes, and cleared his throat. Ultimately, he decided to go with his instincts.

"Honey, I think I need to play by myself for now."

She stood motionless and gave him a stare that he did not recognize. Surely she couldn't be taking it hard? It was only a game, after all. She flipped her sunglasses back over her eyes, pivoted on her left foot, started to turn away, then turned back to him, opened her mouth slightly, and did not speak. She walked backwards one step, smiled, and said, "All right. Go ahead, I guess," and walked off. He watched her go. She stole one more look back at him before entering the house.

There was something about Jeeves' way of expressing himself that struck Gorgoni's funny bone. Bertie had just protested, as Jeeves tried to adjust his employer's tie, that in a crisis ties do not matter, to which Jeeves had replied, "There is no time when ties do not matter, sir." Gorgoni could not contain his laughter at the imagined exchange.

"Remember, we've got the Monroe County barbecue tomorrow," Caroline said, getting into bed beside him.

"Ah, shit. What time?"

"Noon."

"We have to go?"

She dismissed the question with a look. Of course, they had to go.

"Do I have to wear a tie?"

"Of course not. You never wear a tie to the barbecue."

He returned to Bertie's travails, convinced that his wife was in denial about his political future, still unable to entertain a deviation from the most routine of obligations.

"What are you reading?"

"P.G. Wodehouse. *Jeeves and the Tie That Binds*. Very light, silly stuff."

"Well, that's good, for a change. Nice break from energy efficiency studies."

He reread the line about the ties, imagined a formal throwback of a butler delivering it, and succumbed again to nearly helpless giggling.

"I think this is the best book I ever read!" he said.

Caroline looked at him with concern.

"Shut the light," she said.

The pungent smell of grilled flesh permeated the air at the Twenty-Fourth Annual Monroe County Democratic Club Summer Barbecue. A tent had been pitched on the expansive front lawn, under which an impressive array of greasy food was being served, while a local band played soft rock—a medley of James Taylor, Carly Simon, and Judy Collins—on a makeshift stage separated from the food area by a massive oak. The barbecue was a dependably modest fundraiser that had never failed to signal a tedious start to their last sixteen summers. For the last several years, the event was held at the estate of a hedge fund manager who had purchased, on behalf of his parents, one of Bloomington's few authentic mansions. Gorgoni had met the hedge fund manager only twice, and each time was struck by how thoroughly unassuming, unprepossessing and in all ways unremarkable a self-made billionaire could be. His parents, on the other hand, impressed Gorgoni as genuine people of some depth, who seemed bewildered by their son's success and a touch embarrassed at their living arrangements. Upon arriving late at the event, Gorgoni mumbled an excuse to Caroline and headed in the direction of the massive house, where he might escape the crowd for as long as possible.

Caroline sat under an umbrella beside the official hosts, the parents of the hedge fund manager. The three of them had a long, bleak discussion about journalism, about how technology was costing people jobs, and how there seemed to be no remedy for progress. Somehow this led the billionaire's mother, who gravitated to the upbeat, to demonstrate to Caroline how her exciting new smart phone worked. "And then I can go to the Internet like this…" the matronly woman said, tapping on the screen of her new toy. "No, like this…no…"

Her husband, a round-faced, bald gentleman with wire frame glasses, corrected her gently. "You have to use the Google application."

"No, it's got nothing to do with Google; this is for the Internet where we go surfing."

Tommy McCabe, the jowly, pock-marked, garrulous Democratic County Chairman, approached in uncharacteristic haste. His thinning, dark hair was unruly, and one eye opened more widely than the other.

"Caroline, I'd like to begin the festivities, but I don't know where the congressman is."

"I saw him walk towards the house some time ago. He hasn't come out?"

"No one has seen him."

"I assumed he was mingling somewhere."

"Not unless he's mingling in that treehouse," he said, pointing to a tiny treehouse of pine ensconced about fifteen feet up a pepper tree. Tommy laughed boisterously at his own Irish wit, for which he had the erroneous impression that he was renowned. Caroline excused herself to wrangle her husband, hoping against hope that she was on solid ground in dismissing the treehouse hypothesis. She headed for the mansion, which resembled nothing so much as the Parthenon on steroids. She found a few people chatting quietly in the expansive foyer. The kitchen had no party-goers in it, only young, bored members of the catering team. She came upon a high-ceilinged den or family room—built for a family of twenty—with a flat-screen television the size of a movie screen; a few familiar local pols sat on leather couches facing it, munching on chips and chewing the political fat, but none had encountered the congressman.

She exited the house through a side door, walked down a nicely landscaped path framed by purple bougainvillea, and knocked on the open door of a guest house that was nearly the size of the Gorgoni's own home. No one answered, but since the door was open, Caroline entered. The guest house appeared to be empty, but as she looked around, calling out her husband's name, she heard sounds emanating from a basement. A boy was shouting excitedly. She opened the door to the basement and, once halfway down the stairs, spotted Gorgoni playing Foosball with a plump ten-year-old boy.

"Evan, what are you doing here?"

"Be right with you."

"They're ready for you to speak."

"A couple more minutes. I'm up four to two."

"Evan—"

"Five wins."

He continued playing, without looking up.

"Folks, at the end of the day, what's truly important? Not politics. No, it's about seeing the light in our children's eyes, getting a lot of deep, healing sleep, and living every waking hour of our lives with passion and *com*passion. We say that time is precious, but we waste time saying it. Life, in the end, is cruelly short. If there is ambition in your soul, however preposterous, give it expression. Go for the thing that sings. Thank you."

Gorgoni had promised to be brief, and in that regard he could only have exceeded expectations. He spoke no more than a minute. But his words could not have been what those gathered for the Twenty-Fourth Annual Monroe County Democratic Club Summer Barbecue expected to hear. One could almost hear the confusion in the polite, scattered applause that greeted his rather abrupt bounding from the makeshift stage.

"He doesn't seem himself," Caroline said to Tommy McCabe.

"He's probably just a little worn out," Tommy said.

"Yeah." Caroline didn't sound convinced.

"How are the kids?"

"Fine. I think. When we get home, I'll check the light in their eyes."

She excused herself and walked towards the massive oak, under which Gorgoni chatted with a pasty-faced woman of seventy sporting a button that announced her to be a proud Democrat, punctuating the declaration with an exclamation point.

"What are we going to do about the health care crisis?" the proud Democrat asked, cheap red wine on her breath. "It's so discouraging, even after Obamacare. Everyone I know is sick and the costs are so high."

Gorgoni nodded sympathetically. "I'd like to see people eat more shiitake mushrooms," he said.

"Honey, we should go." Caroline took him by the arm, as the proud Democrat squinted at him. Gorgoni gestured a reluctant good-bye to his interlocutor, and walked off with his wife, who seemed suddenly and uncharacteristically more eager than he to return home.

"I've done my best to represent the people of the Ninth District of Indiana for what will be sixteen years by the end of my term. But it's time for new blood. I will not seek re-election next year. I'll take questions now."

The cameras flashed; the reporters' raised voices merged into a cacophony from which the voice of one woman, a stringer for the Indianapolis Star, emerged distinguishable.

"Congressman, is your health an issue here, after your recent hospitalization?"

"No, my health is fine."

"Did you get a diagnosis?"

"*Non-specific vasovagal syncope*—that's the precise medical term for the doctors have no clue why I passed out."

"Are you worried about the Democrats' chances nationally?"

"Haven't thought about it. Because I don't want to have another non-specific vasovagal syncope."

That brought on some chuckles from the reporters, who took turns now shouting out. There were enough of them to practically fill up his entire field office.

"Are you considering a run for the Senate?"

"No."

"Are you ruling it out?"

"Yes."

"Will you definitely serve out your term?"

"Yes."

"What are you going to do next?"

"The family's going to try a new Japanese place on Kirkwood that's supposed to be eclectic."

Why did there have to be a television set, and often several television sets, playing in virtually every restaurant and bar that he set foot in? It was disturbing. At least this one was muted, but he couldn't comprehend why people, while dining, needed to watch what they were watching now: cars chasing each other silently around a track.

"I'll bet it's going to be weird when you go back to Washington now," Nicole said, serving herself some mashed Japanese sweet potatoes. "You're going to be like a lame duck."

"Let me go with you for a week," Caroline said, sipping her miso soup.

"Why?" Gorgoni said, examining vegetables he did not recognize on his macrobiotic plate.

"For the taping, and to hang out a little in D.C."

The taping. He had almost forgotten about *Meet the Press*. They had called to book him as soon as he had announced the press conference. It was, after all, a slow news season. "Okay," he said. "Mandy, take care of your sister for a week. Grandma will look in on you."

Caroline's mother could always be counted on to help out, and she lived only two miles away.

"Does it have to be a whole week?" Nicole said.

"Shut up or you're grounded," Mandy said.

Nicole looked worried. "Are you really going to go back to teaching?" she asked her father.

"I don't know," Gorgoni said. "I'd like to help kids somehow." Nicole shook her head, apparently stunned. "You look disappointed," he said.

"Isn't teacher, like, a lower job than congressman?" she said.

"It's the other way around, Nicole," he said.

"Would you rather be a teacher or a principal?" Mandy said.

"Teacher," he said. "Being principal can lead to politics. If only I had known it at the time…"

He tried to meditate, to think of nothing at all, as the make-up woman applied a brush to his face. It had become, over the years, a superstition with him: thinking too hard before a television appearance inevitably resulted in stumbles. It was more important for him to be emotionally composed than to know precisely what he wanted to say. The only thing he let himself think about was what might be going through Caroline's mind as she sat in a corner of the room, watching him.

"Have you done *Meet the Press* before, Congressman?" asked the make-up woman.

"Three or four times," he said.

"Is it still a thrill?" she said.

"Tell me you're kidding," he said.

No more than five minutes later he found himself seated in a bright studio opposite Chuck Todd, the cameras looming over them, and then their red lights on.

Into the camera, Chuck Todd introduced Gorgoni as a "distinguished, moderate, and collegial" member of Congress, then turned to him to begin the questioning with a predictable opener: "Congressman Gorgoni, why are you retiring?"

Of course he knew the question was coming, but he had decided what he would say only during the introduction.

"Chuck, when I first came to Washington, I was as eager as a Little Leaguer pitching his first game. It's a decade and a half later, we've had Republican presidents, Democratic presidents, Republican Congresses, Democratic Congresses, and I don't see any improvement. I have nothing to say to my constituents other than I'm profoundly sorry. So I'll hang up my cleats and—"

"But you're only one member of Congress out of five hundred thirty-five."

Chuck Todd, who was a nice guy, seemed to be offering him absolution. Gorgoni looked him in the eye like he was confiding in a friend.

"That's what we all tell ourselves, but who's to blame but us? So, no, I'm not going to pass the buck."

"Has the partisan atmosphere become so intense that you've given up on Congress as an institution?"

"Let's just say that, on a personal level, I yearn for comity. And after a decade and a half in Washington, I ache to live somewhere where I can find it. I don't think that's a weakness, but if it is, so be it."

"Turning to foreign affairs, tensions are rising again now with Iran. Some argue that it's time for strong action. Do you think the president should keep all options, including military strikes, on the table?"

"Chuck, I have an irrational brother-in-law; I used to try to reason with him—he wound up institutionalized, unfortunately—but when you negotiate with irrationality, there is no right answer. You do the best you can."

In the green room, Caroline watched the screen, munching on crudités. She paused with a baby carrot between her teeth as her brother earned a mention as a parallel to a terrorist state.

"So all options should be on the table?" Chuck Todd went on.

"You do the best you can."

"But you would not be supportive of military action?"

Gorgoni smiled in admiration of his interlocutor's persistence.

"You know, I'm one-eighth Native American—Lakota—on my mother's side. There's no eighth of me that I'm more proud of. And the Lakota had a war custom called *counting coup*—all you had to do was touch the enemy with a stick, without any harm coming to anyone, and you won that point in battle. Now if that was still how humanity waged war, I'd sooner consider it as an option."

"As the ranking Democratic member of the Energy and Commerce Committee, you wrote legislation to try to cap carbon emissions, legislation that has stalled so far. What do you see as its chances?"

April Madrue had urged him to maintain an air of cautious optimism on the issue, in case the political climate changed, but he didn't find the rationale persuasive.

"Not a chance in hell."

"That's pretty blunt."

"People can't see carbon dioxide, can't see methane, can't see how they cause climate change. But they fear job losses, and fear trumps abstractions. Fear is visceral; abstractions are intellectual."

"You've also worked on an education bill, which would increase funding for magnet schools and for arts education, and for the repair of decaying school buildings."

"It's not going to pass in this atmosphere of austerity."

"How do you turn that around?"

"It would require a sudden realization by the Members of Congress that the education of our children will offer more security to our future than the latest weapons program. I don't see that happening anytime soon. I don't remember the last time any single Member had a revelation on that scale."

"As you know, many states and localities, hampered by budgetary shortfalls, have been cutting back on education, laying off teachers."

"The responsibility to educate the next generation should be solemn. Unlike, say, the obligation to incarcerate people who have inhaled the smoke of the burning leaves of an illegal plant."

"Turning then to the fiscal situation, can the president and Congress ever bring the budget into balance?"

Gorgoni shook his head. "It's too easy politically to cut taxes and too hard to cut spending. The budget isn't going to begin to move in the right direction until we put millions of Americans back to work."

"Does that mean another jobs bill, or—?"

"We're bleeding jobs. Exporting them to countries where they've got millions of people willing to work for wages far below what supports middle-class Americans."

"How do we stop that?"

Gorgoni looked at Chuck Todd warmly, as if he were a good friend, and momentarily held his two empty palms outstretched, like a man hoping for rain. "You got me. Truth is, you can't say it, but there are too many people in the world. From the era of Jesus to the era of George Washington, the population of the world increased by about five hundred million. In my lifetime, it's increased by over four billion, and I take a lot of supplements so if I'm lucky, and the planet is not, I may live to see a few more billion. Does anyone seriously believe that that's sustainable? If civilization keeps procreating this way, we're doomed."

He saw that Chuck Todd sported an uncharacteristic expression of surprise.

"Doomed by population growth?" Chuck Todd said.

"Among other things, but it all stems from that, yes. That shouldn't be a controversial statement. Ask those who disagree how the earth can sustain a population of twenty billion people. The time for being fruitful and multiplying has long since passed. It made sense when that book was written, not now."

"Do you have anything uplifting to say, Congressman? Anything positive?"

"Yes, Chuck, I do. I attended a Correspondents' Dinner after-party back in May, and you are a remarkably good dancer."

Chuck Todd beamed. "We'll let that be the last word. Thank you, Congressman, for joining us today."

Caroline did not greet him as he entered the green room; her head was down as she sat at the end of a beige couch. That was unlike her. Even when he had flubbed the yuan devaluation question, years ago, she had been remarkably supportive. This time she seemed stung.

"Was that for my benefit?" she asked, softly, without raising her eyes.

"What do you mean?"

"You wanted to make it abundantly clear that you're done with politics? In case I harbored any illusions?"

"It had nothing to do with you, Caroline."

"You compared Iran to my brother."

Gorgoni tilted his head to one side and nodded, granting the point.

"The words popped into my head."

"You pissed on your own record."

"Man, that was liberating."

They sat in the green room and watched the next segment of the show being taped. Chuck Todd sat around a table with Joe Klein, Andrew Sullivan, and Arianna Huffington. The three men wore conservative, dark suits, although Klein's alone was striped; Arianna Huffington contrasted with them in a striking teal blouse and oval gold earrings of impressive size.

"Congressman Gorgoni made the case that many of our problems simply can't be solved," Chuck Todd said. "I've never heard a politician speak that way before."

"It was strange and oddly endearing," Joe Klein said. "Here was a guy kind of throwing up his hands and saying, '*I don't know what to do about this.*'"

"I kept thinking how sad it was," Arianna Huffington said. "He truly sealed his political fate today."

Andrew Sullivan's British accent served only to heighten the tone of cheer that he brought to his words: "But how refreshing to hear a politician say he's quitting and it's not to spend time with his family!"

Arianna Huffington chimed in with a smile: "And this is one of the few people on the Hill who actually would like to spend time with his family. He's one of the most respected legislators in Congress—"

"Indeed," said Andrew Sullivan.

"What did you make of his odd metaphor," asked Chuck Todd, "in relation to tensions in the Middle East, of dealing with a mentally ill brother-in-law?"

Chuck Todd appeared to have stumped his panel. For a long moment, there was no response at all. It may have been a first in Sunday morning round tables.

"I thought it was on the mark," Andrew Sullivan said at last. "Iran *is* like your crazy brother-in-law."

Gorgoni resisted the impulse to cast a glance of vindication at his wife. He kept his gaze on the television screen.

"You know, politicians make an art form of humility," Joe Klein was saying, "and it's usually fake. They say, 'I'm just a plain old mill worker's son,' then build themselves a thirty-thousand-square-foot mansion. But here's a guy, Evan Gorgoni, who is truly humble; he's always sided with working people and he's clearly feeling kind of despondent on their behalf, and with nothing to lose now, he's speaking from the heart."

Caroline stood up to leave. "Don't gloat," she said. "You got lucky."

They left the Nebraska Avenue studio in their Prius, with Caroline insisting on driving, although not explaining why. It was a short ride on Van Ness Street to Connecticut Avenue, and from there a smooth and pleasant ride home to Gorgoni's apartment on Columbia Road NW. The Adams Morgan neighborhood appealed to Gorgoni; it was hip, lively, and multi-ethnic, and boasted the best restaurants and bars in town. He probably had dined on Ethiopian food more often than any other Hoosier of his acquaintance. There was a lot about life in Washington, D.C., that he would miss; in fact, nearly everything that didn't involve Capitol Hill. But too many of his hours were lost on the Hill; he never had enough time to create a life for himself in the neighborhood in which he ostensibly lived.

They eschewed the elevator and walked up the stairs to the second floor apartment overlooking Kalorama Park. They found Jake lying on his back on the white divan in the living room, a book lifted over his face with one hand while he petted his unusually blotchy calico cat, Filibuster, curled up on the floor, with the other. Jake bounded to his feet to greet Caroline.

"Hey, what's a woman doing in our bachelor pad?" he said, and gave her a quick embrace.

"How's the congressman from cheese?" Caroline said.

"Your husband refuses to vote for my dairy subsidy," Jake said, in a tone of mock outrage.

"Evan, how can you vote against your own roommate?"

"It would be good for him," Gorgoni said, "but would it be good for the cows?"

"I was with you on campaign finance reform," Jake said. "I should have made it a *quid pro quo*."

"Too late," Gorgoni said. "I think it was Caligula who said, '*No quid pro quos ex post facto, amicus*.'"

"You've got to play hardball with Evan," Caroline said.

"After that performance on *Meet the Press*, I don't think he's making any deals," Jake said.

"Let's get something to eat, shall we?" Gorgoni said.

They walked to *Paros*, a Greek place where, over plates of braised dandelion, roasted potatoes, tzatziki, hummus, baba ganoush, and spiced olives, they waxed collectively nostalgic over their early years in politics.

"So I'm fresh out of college, canvassing for Harris," Jake said. "Sweet man, popular in Green Bay, but a lush. Which we were told to deny vehemently. So I knock on the door of a log cabin—"

"A real log cabin?" Caroline asked.

"Who the hell knows? It's real in my memory," Jake said. "So I knock on the door, and this red-haired Irish guy answers the door, and says, *'This Harris feller, he's a drinker, isn't he?'*" Jake managed a convincing brogue. "*'No, no, no,'* I say, *'that's all trumped up! Harris never touches the stuff!' 'Ah, well, then the hell with 'im!'* And the guy slams the door in my face!"

Caroline smiled. There was nothing she loved more than political war stories. But the sadness behind the smile bespoke her acceptance that their days in the heart of the political world were numbered.

"We had one of Evan's first fundraisers in our living room," she said, "and the founding partner of a Bloomington law firm was there. We're plying him with liquor, and I'm kind of flirting—"

"You flirted with Don?" Gorgoni asked.

"Not in a sexual way," Caroline said.

"How else do you flirt?"

"Monetarily."

"You can't flirt monetarily!"

"You can when you're down by five."

"Flirting monetarily!" Gorgoni said, with a harrumph.

Caroline brushed her bangs off her eyes and turned back to Jake. "So I'm buttering up this ambulance chaser, and he asks me how Evan feels about tort reform. Evan walks over with his usual flare for timing and announces that he's open to it, that something needs to be done. The guy stares at him like he's seen a ghost, but says he so respects Evan's character and honesty—"

"He gives us a check," Gorgoni said.

"A thousand bucks. We were really touched by that," Caroline said, and as if she still was, her eyes grew a little misty.

"Until the check bounced," Gorgoni said, sopping up some hummus with the last remaining half of pita bread in their basket. He then requested another round of Guinness beers and more pita bread from a lanky waitress with a silver nose ring, a Georgetown T-shirt, and a clump of electric pink in her straight black hair.

"He put a stop payment on it," Caroline said.

"He'd thought it over," Gorgoni explained, "and decided that stopping tort reform trumped character."

Jake beamed. "Beautiful."

"It was like an initiation," Gorgoni said.

"Yup," Jake said. "We survive those, we get sucked in by the influence, and soon the game's too heady for most mortals to give up."

"Yeah," Gorgoni mumbled.

"But not for you. Why'd you do it, Ev?"

Gorgoni felt that he owed his friend an answer. But there was no answer that came readily to his lips. Why did he do it? Why did he jettison a political life he had fought so hard to obtain? What was this instinct that seemed to be controlling him now, protecting him now, against every conscious plan he and Caroline had painstakingly hatched during the whole of their married lives? Why did he do it?

"When I was a little kid," Gorgoni said, "my father finally relented after a lot of begging and said we could get a dog. At the pound. So we took a trip there and I got to choose which dog's life to save. And I knew that whatever dog I chose, I'd be condemning all the others to death. I was paralyzed."

Gorgoni stopped right there and tapped the table with his fingers. He looked off into the distance and smiled. Jake was not about to accept that that was the end of the story. "So what kind of dog did you get?" he asked, a touch of annoyance in his voice.

The new round of beers arrived and Gorgoni took a long draught from his glass mug. Then he put the mug down and looked straight ahead.

"We didn't get a dog," he said, at last.

Caroline ran her hand through her husband's hair. "I wish you'd told me that story before you ran for office," she said, with something resembling sorrow in her eyes.

Their car trip to Ronald Reagan Airport was a quiet one. Gorgoni remembered how, early in the marriage, silences had felt uncomfortable to him; then, once there were two children in the house, silences were blessed, rare occurrences. This silence in the car was the first in memory that seemed uncomfortable again. There had been no fight; there had been only a kind of quiet parting of the ways. They no longer saw their future through the same eyes, not since he had decided that he was done with politics. He felt tension in the air, but it was tension absent conflict, which made it that much harder to address.

At the gate, as he dropped her off for her flight to Indianapolis, he gave her an unusually tight hug. She reciprocated with a wan smile.

"See you in three weeks. Try to lay low, okay?" she said.

"What do you mean?"

"No more interviews. Just go to committee meetings and keep your nose to the grindstone."

"I'll work hard. That could be part of what it means to go for the thing that—"

"You know you can't carry a tune," she said peremptorily, and boarded the plane.

Caroline sat in coach next to a garrulous, fiftyish woman who ran a dental office. As soon as the woman learned that Caroline was a lawyer, she confided that she was considering suing her landlord, and asked for Caroline's card.

"Right when I need a lawyer, that's really lucky," the woman said. She put on a pair of glasses to read the card. "Caroline Finley-Gorgoni? Are you Congressman Gorgoni's wife, by any chance?"

"Yes."

The woman lit up. "He's my congressman. It's an irony, I've got to say. I have to admit, I never voted for him before, but I would now. But now he's not running!"

Caroline found herself intrigued by the comment.

"Why, uh, why did your opinion change?"

"I saw him on *Meet the Press*."

"Uh-huh."

"He doesn't talk down to you. What a breath of fresh air. I'm so sick of the childishness in Washington, and your husband may be the only adult in the room."

Caroline smiled and nodded.

Gorgoni knew that he should prepare for a subcommittee meeting the next day on natural gas fracking, but he couldn't resist the temptation to relax on the couch and watch some television. The only television he generally enjoyed was oddball programming on cable stations like Animal Planet or the History Channel. He channel-surfed until he ran across a program called, "Earth, The Volatile Planet," joining it twenty minutes late. A tall, skinny Brit wearing glasses and a wrinkled white shirt was standing in front of Old Faithful.

"Two of the most spectacular and deadly volcanic eruptions in the past few million years have come from right here at Yellowstone. If Yellowstone were to blow again, thick ash deposits would all but bury the United States, disrupt the earth's climate, and threaten life as we know it on the planet. Yellowstone has been on a regular eruption cycle of roughly six hundred thousand years, with the last eruption occurring some six hundred forty thousand years ago."

Jake walked into the living room from his bedroom.

"I just got off the phone with the Whip. I can't believe we're going to have another damned vote on school vouchers."

"At the moment, I'm more concerned with supervolcanoes."

"Huh?"

"I'm watching this show, it's devastating. Did you know that if the supervolcano in Yellowstone blows, that's the end of humanity?"

Jake's forehead had a way of breaking into a thick series of wrinkles whenever he raised his eyebrows in confusion or wonder, as he did now.

"So?"

"What do you mean, so?"

"That's Wyoming."

"Yeah?"

"That's a red state."

Gorgoni waved his hand in the air as if to erase Jake's comment. "You missed my point," he said, then spoke slowly and emphatically. "It's the end of life on earth."

"You missed my point," Jake said. "It gets them first."

At Bloomington High North, Mandy was taking summer courses in Computer Applications and Spanish, beefing up her academic resume before next year's college applications. She cherished her lunch breaks. She always brought a sandwich from home, usually homemade sunflower pâté with alfalfa sprouts on rye, and she sat with a new group of friends, a refreshing change from the friends she normally sat with during the regular school year; these half-dozen new friends, half male, half female, were quirkier, less popular, and more interested in the wider world than in who was dating whom. And between them they sported three nose studs, four eyebrow studs, a tongue stud, and more earrings than she could count. Today she was the last to arrive at the table, and found them all abuzz with a *YouTube* video.

She joined three of her friends in leaning over the shoulders of Frazier, a gawky, six-foot-three computer genius who was seated at the table, hunched over an AP Calculus book and managing to study despite the commotion. On his iPad she saw a full-screen image of her father. It was from his interview on *Meet the Press* that she had forgotten to watch on Sunday. "...From the era of Jesus to the era of George Washington, the population of the world increased by about five hundred million. In my lifetime, it's increased by over four billion..." Her friends were emitting *wows* and cheers. Nikki, her soft-spoken new friend who always wore denim overalls and a lot of black mascara around her blue eyes, turned to her with a wide grin.

"Mandy, your dad is so cool."

"He is, isn't he?" Mandy said.

"Everyone was talking about him at the *Runcible Spoon*," Nikki said, referring to a venerable local café.

Frazier looked up at Mandy. Was it a twitch or was it possible that such a nerdy guy winked at her? "Way cool," he said.

Caroline sat on the wood-framed, brown tweed couch in the cozy Gorgoni den, a plate of date confections before her on the beaten-up walnut coffee table, and watched *The Situation Room* on CNN.

"Our lead story today," Wolf Blitzer was saying, in his patented way of imparting a controlled urgency to his voice without altering his facial expression a whit, "...is a video that's gone viral. Retiring Indiana Congressman Evan Gorgoni gave an interview that some call fatalistic and others praise as refreshingly open and honest. On *YouTube,* over two and a half million people have watched the interview in just twenty-four hours. We'll be discussing the implications with the best political team on television…"

She ate without looking at her treats, chewing mechanically, absorbed in the spectacle that her husband presented on the screen, wondering if it could really be possible that so many people found inspiration in what she had considered an act of political suicide. Usually, her political instincts were dead-on. But even if she had been wrong, what difference did it make? Her husband was clearly no longer interested in, or emotionally capable of, seizing political opportunity, even if one improbably existed in the fractured *zeitgeist*. All the same, she hoped she had been wrong.

Of the evening news broadcasts, Jake always watched only the NBC Nightly News because the local NBC affiliate in Green Bay had been the first to declare him the winner in his first Congressional election, nine years ago; Jake was nothing if not loyal. Besides, Brian Williams, whom he had met on a couple of occasions socially, seemed like a guy he could gladly knock down some beers with on a summer evening.

"There's a buzz in Washington, D.C. and throughout the country tonight," Brian Williams was saying. "Specifically, what was Congressman Evan Gorgoni up to when he appeared to be saying that we're doomed? Chuck Todd has the story."

"Evan!" Jake called.

Trusty little green-handled scissors in hand, Gorgoni emerged from the bathroom, where he had been snipping his mustache. On the screen he saw a clip from his *Meet the Press* interview.

"If civilization keeps procreating this way, we're doomed."

Chuck Todd looked as awkward and vulnerable as ever, standing in front of the Capitol with a mic in his hand, his mouth open for a moment or two before any words emerged, his eyes blinking rapidly; but when he spoke at last, a tone of confidence emerged.

"Retiring Congressman Evan Gorgoni has suddenly burst onto the national scene. Millions who missed my interview with him on *Meet the Press* have since watched it online. Bloggers are posting furiously about what *The Daily Kos* has called, or coined, *The Politics of Acceptance*. *Politico* is reporting a new surge of interest in the congressman's political future, though none of that interest seems to be coming from the congressman himself. His office has no comment. Some are speculating that he might run for the Senate or even the White House. By most accounts, Senator Nate Poston of New Hampshire appears poised for a cakewalk to the Democratic nomination, facing only a spirited but under-funded challenge from Senator Carl Oakley of Missouri. That leaves a lot of Democrats wishing for a third option. The question they're asking, Brian, is: could Evan Gorgoni be that Democratic savior?"

Gorgoni grabbed the remote from Jake's hand and shut off the TV. Jake was grinning his extra-wide grin, which was his substitute for a laugh.

"Jolene already called to tell me to tell you to go for it," he said, referring to his wife.

"I've been called a lot of things in my life, but never savior."

"Frankly, I'd been thinking that you'd taken leave of your senses, but apparently everyone else has, too, so it could work for you."

"Geez, what does a guy have to do to get laid off in this town?"

"Keep me in mind for a Cabinet post."

Gorgoni's iPhone rang, to the opening bars of Bruce Springsteen's *American Land*. He looked at the call screen; it was Mandy. He picked up the phone, which was resting on the wet-bar.

"Mandy?"

"Dad, have you seen—?"

It wasn't the best of connections; there was some static on the line. He thought he heard the sounds of traffic.

"Yeah."

"Are you going to run for president?"

"No, it's preposterous. You're not driving, are you?"

"No. Wait a minute, I want you to hear this."

She handed her cell to Frazier, who was driving.

"Congressman, it's an honor—"

"Who's this?"

"Frazier Milner, sir. I'm taking your lovely and fully intact daughter to the movies now to see a family-friendly, PG-rated film, and I want you to know that I'll be eighteen in time for the next president—"

"I think you mean election."

"Right you are, the next election, and I'd vote for you and my parents said they'd vote for you and by the way, we're Republicans, but we believe in science and stuff like that."

"Okay, could you put Mandy back on and concentrate on your driving?"

"Yes, sir, it's been an honor, sir. And I just want to say that party or ideology doesn't mean as much to me as being a truth-teller and a wisdom-seeker."

"Yeah, give me Mandy."

"Here she is, sir, as pure as the driven snow."

Mandy took the phone back. She was very pleased with how respectful her date had sounded.

"Pretty cool, huh, Dad?"

"You're dating a Republican?"

"Yeah, I guess. Is that a problem?"

"No. If he tries anything, remember, you can filibuster. Your mother can explain."

Walking into the Rayburn Congressional building didn't confer the thrill that it once had. He had actually interned in the same building the summer when he was twenty, in the office of Congressman Lee Hamilton, when the building felt so marvelously hip, and when a ride in the subway tunnel to the Capitol felt like he'd been initiated into a secret passage to the heart of democracy. Hamilton remained his model of what a congressman should be: sensible, informed, steady, caring. If only there were 435 Lee Hamiltons, he used to say, whatever their ideology, if they simply had the humanity and civility of Lee Hamilton, they would get along and the country would fare well. But now Congress was run by ideologues, many with ideologies that might be popular in their own district but not in the country at large, and getting along was simply not among their goals. Despite the building's airy charm, Rayburn had become a hostile work environment.

Upon entering his Congressional suite, he was greeted by Emma Livingston, who had been his receptionist since his first day on the job fifteen years ago. Emma was an African-American woman of almost his age, with a short, plump body and an angular face with far-apart eyes. Her particular charm was that you could never tell when she was joking.

"Morning, Congressman. You have requests for interviews from *Time, Newsweek, Washington Post, Nightline, CBS, NBC, CNN, Politico*—shall I go on?

"Turn them all down. Emergency staff meeting in my office in five minutes."

"You got it. Senator Poston wants to meet with you here at two o'clock; I confirmed."

"Poston? Oh, Christ. What does he want?"

"What do you think?"

"The man's got no subtlety."

"You know, I didn't know you were part—what tribe was it again?"

"Lakota. My mother's grandmother."

"How come you never mentioned that before?"

"The subject never came up."

"It's a real selling point! You should emphasize it in your presidential campaign."

"There's not going to be any—"

"Okay, but if you do run, use the Native American thing."

"How?"

"*Gorgoni for President. Take back America!*" She paused for emphasis. "That should attract the Native American vote."

He looked at her closely. There was no smile. You just couldn't tell.

"Staff meeting. Five minutes," he said.

With all of the staff assembled in his inner office, Gorgoni stood and wondered for a moment what exactly he should say.

They were all looking at him a little funny, with expectant eyes. Something must have been in the coffee this morning.

"I'm sorry," he said. "You were all the ones I wanted to tell first, but of course you can't conduct business that way in this town. So I'm sorry you all learned of my plans through the media. I'll serve out this term, of course—we still have almost a year and a half to go, so you've got plenty of notice—but it will be my last. I'll do my best to make sure that you all land on your feet. There isn't a person in this room to whom I won't give a stellar recommendation. It's been an honor to work with all of you, and I hope you'll continue to work with me for the remainder of the term, but I certainly won't blame any of you if you seize another opportunity. And in case you're wondering, no, I'm not running for president, so rule that out as a potential source of employment."

April Madrue, who had squeezed herself into one of the office armchairs, said, "There's still a lot we can accomplish in the time we have left!" April was always optimistic to a fault.

Mona, a legislative aide who was his newest hire, and already as brash as anyone on the staff, piped up.

"Why won't you run? We don't want to have to choose between a wimp like Poston and—"

"First of all, Senator Poston may not be the nominee," Gorgoni said. "Second, he's going to be here this afternoon, so let's be careful what we say. I would object to that characterization."

"You're the only one who can stop him," Mona said.

"I don't believe that's true. Who in this room believes that's true?"

Every hand went up.

"Would you like me to count the votes?" Emma said, to all appearances serious, her arm raised.

Caroline liked to grocery shop at *Bloomingfoods* cooperative, where she could get organic produce, and where the atmosphere was funky and down-home. There was a sense of community there that you couldn't find in a commercial grocery store. She almost always ran into someone she knew, and today was no exception. Amy Wintergarden, a schoolteacher about ten years her junior but with a daughter the same age as Nicole, said hello as Caroline was selecting some zucchinis.

"Amy, good to see you. How's Gina?"

"Everyone's good; the divorce is final," Amy said.

"I know it's tough but I'm sure it was for the best."

Amy beamed at her.

"I signed the petition online today."

"You had to sign a petition to get a divorce?"

"No, urging Evan to run for president. I remember when he was principal, I was thinking he'd make a good president."

"The whole thing's crazy," Caroline said.

"Actually, the status quo is what's crazy," Amy said. "Breaking the status quo is the hardest thing to do, but I can tell you from personal experience, it feels great."

And with that, Amy pushed on with her shopping cart.

"Senator Poston is here." Emma's voice came through the speakerphone crisply. Scarcely a moment after Gorgoni told her to send him in, there was a perfunctory knock on the door and Nate Poston entered. He was a tall man, about six foot one, with silver hair, an aquiline nose, and a dimpled chin. The only thing that kept him from perfectly presidential looks was the five o'clock shadow that never went away, and that seemed perfectly consistent with his deep voice and testosterone-fueled personality.

"Hello, Evan," Poston said.

"Nate, good to see you."

Gorgoni emerged from behind his desk to shake the senator's hand. There were two armchairs facing Gorgoni's desk. Gorgoni sat in one, and gestured for Poston to sit in the other.

"I just met with Prince Charles," Poston said, as he sat down.

"Did you?" Gorgoni said.

"Very down-to-earth guy, for a prince."

"That's what I hear."

"He kept talking about natural farming. I think he would have become a farmer himself if he hadn't settled on, you know, prince."

"Uh-huh."

"Highly concerned about hoof-and-mouth disease. It's a real passion for him."

"Why'd you want to see me, Nate?"

He noticed that Poston seemed pleased with his bluntness. Schmoozing didn't come easily with the senator. Poston leaned forward and placed his hands on his knees.

"I'd like your support, Evan. Assuming, of course, that you're not running yourself."

"I'm not. That's all wild speculation, out of my control."

"Well, if you want to stop it, endorse me and the subject is closed. And no promises, of course, but you'd be on anyone's short list for Energy Secretary. And I'm not going to forget the ones who back me early."

Where do you get that from? Gorgoni thought. *Where do you get the confidence of the anointed?*

"What would your energy policy be?"

The question seemed to take Poston aback for a moment.

"As president?"

"As president."

"Well, it would be—you know as well as anyone—our energy profile changes, you have to be flexible, and I'd support all measures that are necessary and sustainable. As long as they're affordable. More wind, more solar, more natural gas, clean coal, some conservation. And of course we can't leave oil and nuclear out of the equation. And we have to modernize the grid. You can't take the drill everywhere approach, but you also can't put up too many obstacles to drilling. It's got to be handled intelligently. I'll bring a nuanced approach."

Poston looked at him with curiosity, as if he didn't expect to be grilled but didn't want to offend. He wore an expression of discomfort.

"Why do you want to be president, Nate?" Gorgoni thought it was a fair question to ask.

Poston crossed one leg over the other and rubbed his ankle. He looked long and hard at Gorgoni and seemed to need to satisfy himself that the congressman wasn't putting him on. Then he leaned back.

"That's uh, you know, that's the sort of question that, if you really want a specific, for example, just now talking with the prince, things come up that if you're president, you can speak with authority on all kinds of matters that can move the country forward. It isn't about me—I don't have to tell you that, Evan. It's, you know, who's right for the country. To get out in front of history, instead of it just happening, and we're left holding the bag. If we can lift Americans' spirits, I truly believe we can become a shining city on a hill. I really do."

Gorgoni was overtaken by a wave of nausea. He couldn't help but stare at the senator, and he couldn't help it if his look betrayed his fear.

In the Congressional gym, Gorgoni ran on the treadmill with an intensity bordering on the maniacal. His previous record was four hundred eighty-five calories burned in one session, set the day his education bill failed to get out of committee. He now had surpassed five hundred. He would shoot for six hundred. He was sweating profusely. As he wiped his cheeks dry, he wondered if the moisture was sweat or tears; it was hard to tell if he was crying. All he knew was that he didn't want to get off the machine. Then, and only then, he would have to face the question of what to do next. The machine groaned as he increased the slope of the incline, and picked up the pace.

"The man must be stopped," Gorgoni said. He was on the landline in his apartment, set to speaker, as he washed down with ionized spring water his CoQ10, his ginkgo biloba, and his hawthorn.

"Look, I was never a big fan of Poston's, but he's all right," Caroline said.

"Try to get a straight answer out of the guy—it's like trying to hit a hummingbird from thirty yards with a paper plane."

"He's cautious. That's what's gotten him this far."

"He said if he's elected, we could be a shining city on a hill."

Caroline stopped herself in the midst of serving chilled cucumber soup for Nicole, Mandy, and herself.

"He said that?"

"Where the hell is this hill, anyway?"

"He really said that?"

"He's got to be stopped. He's telling me what he can do for the country, I'm looking in his eyes, and I swear I could see out the back of his head."

"Well, maybe Carl can stop him."

"Carl's a womanizing showboat who they say doesn't even show up for committee meetings."

"I know. If only there were more women on the committees…"

Gorgoni gazed wistfully out the window at Kalorama Park. He would gladly do no more than sit in the park and play chess with the locals.

"Honey, I'm sorry, but I think I have to run for president. I think that's how I go for the thing that—"

Caroline ran into the kitchen with the pitcher full of chilled soup and put it down on the counter, mystifying Mandy, who had not yet been served. She spoke quietly.

"Oh, God, Evan, you can't possibly—"

"I know it's a longshot."

"Forget the odds for a second. Daunting as they are."

"Okay."

"You're not, Evan—you're not up to it now. You need your rest."

"You wanted me to run for re-election."

"I was wrong. I didn't realize—now I see—"

"What changed your mind?"

"You've been a little different. Since the day you passed out."

"Different?"

"Yes."

"Different good or different bad?"

"Wait a minute." With a look of curiosity, Mandy had walked into the kitchen with her bowl. Caroline apologized to her and served her some soup. After Mandy returned, walking backwards at first, to the dining room, Caroline continued, softly: "Different peculiar."

He knew she was feeling that way; it was good to hear her acknowledge it. "Maybe," Gorgoni said. "Something may have happened to me. An alteration of perception."

Caroline was surprised to hear him say it. "You're aware of it, too?"

"Yeah," Gorgoni said. "I feel clearer. Mentally. I think I'm sharper."

She wished he were in the room with her so that she would have a better chance of reaching him. She had little choice now but to resort to logic.

"Poston's got thirty-six million cash on hand and twenty Senate endorsements. Where do you even start?"

"With Monty."

Monty Berg, as Caroline well knew, had long been the one campaign manager in the country whom Gorgoni admired. They had never worked together, but they had once discussed a Senate bid that Gorgoni eventually decided against. And Monty had always been generous with free advice during Gorgoni's Congressional re-election campaigns.

"Monty? He's been out of the game for years."

"Maybe he'd jump back in to run my campaign."

"Didn't I hear that he's in Kentucky, racing horses?"

Gorgoni shook his head.

"No. Louisiana. Dogs."

The racetrack seated several thousand, but only a couple of hundred people were present this balmy evening, cheering wildly as greyhounds raced around the dirt oval aided, or perhaps burdened, by uniformed Capuchin monkeys as jockeys. Gorgoni sat and watched in stunned amazement as Monty, a sloppy, unshaven, balding, jowly man of sixty with a potbelly on which he liked to clasp his hands, gorged on popcorn as he urged on his chosen team of dog-and-monkey. His cheeks were red, the skin peeling from psoriasis, and his front teeth were oversized and crooked.

"People think it's the dog," Monty said, over the crowd noise. "It's not. It's the jockey. A good jockey can ride a four-year-old greyhound and beat a two-year-old. A good jockey can challenge an old dog, make him believe in himself—"

Gorgoni looked nothing if not perplexed.

"But...they're monkeys."

Monty dismissed the comment as parochial.

"Don't hold that against them."

The race ended. A greyhound-and-monkey in a blue uniform sporting the number 19 crossed the finish line. Monty erupted in glee.

"*Jimbo* again! That monkey cannot be stopped! He must win half his races, and even when he loses he finishes in the trifecta. Look how nonchalant he is! I tell you, I'm going to make this an Olympic sport."

Gorgoni gave him a skeptical look.

"Uh, Monty…there are no people involved."

His friend gritted his teeth.

"It's gonna be an uphill fight," Monty said.

When all the excitement was over, all the patrons on their way home, and all the dogs and monkeys returned to their respective paddocks where they spent their evenings attended to by solicitous track personnel, Monty and Gorgoni took a stroll around the dog track. A flock of sparrows flew above, and crickets chirped all around them.

"Do you miss the game?" Gorgoni asked.

"It's a disease," Monty said.

"So you miss it."

"I had candidates paying me three, four hundred grand to run their campaigns. And then I'd go to their events, listen to their pitches for funds, and I'd think, these poor suckers are taking out their checkbooks because they believe in the candidate, but what they're really doing is buying me a huge fucking house. And I'm no saint, but after I got the huge fucking house in New Orleans to give to my ex, I thought maybe enough is enough."

Monty took a bunched-up handkerchief out of his back pocket, unfurled it, and blew his nose.

"You were worth the money."

"Yeah, because I was so good at raising it." He jumbled up the handkerchief and returned it to his back pocket. "Why do you want to be president?"

"I don't."

Monty coughed up some phlegm and spat. "Then why the hell are you—?"

"Because if I don't run, the country's going to choose between another cynical tax-cutter, and Nate Poston. Who has never met a question he couldn't dodge."

Monty smiled. "And you're not going to dodge any?"

"I'm going to face reality. For the hell of it. And try to pull the other guys into the pond with me. Poston's already talking about climate change like a believer, since I did *Meet the Press*."

Monty stared up into the lights of the track.

"You're tempting me."

"Good."

"You know why?"

"Why?"

"Because I'd rather lose and go down swinging than win some tepid, cautious, meaningless victory."

"Hey, if you want to lose, I'm pretty confident I'm your guy."

"Don't get cocky."

"I can't do it without you, Monty."

Monty looked at him skeptically.

"I'm sure you can lose without me."

"Yeah, but not well."

Monty nodded. Then he stopped walking and scratched his head. Gorgoni stopped alongside and looked down at the dirt; the tracks of greyhounds were still fresh. He raised his head as Monty sighed.

"How's your health? You had that incident."

"Excellent."

"Then why'd you pass out?"

"I was apparently very tired."

"You're going to need a better answer than that."

"Dehydration."

"Is that the truth?"

"Have you ever been in a hospital? You can get remarkably bad mashed potatoes there, but you can't get the truth."

"If you have any success in this campaign, eventually you're going to need to show your medical records. You got any problem with that?"

"Not at all. I don't have any records, other than that hospital visit."

"Don't you go for annual physicals?"

"No."

"When was the last time you went for one?"

"Never."

"You're kidding me?"

"No."

"Why don't you go for check-ups?"

"I don't like doctors."

Monty shook his head and blinked rapidly.

"How do you get your prescriptions?"

"I don't have any prescriptions."

Monty nodded. "That would be more impressive if we actually knew anything about your health. Get a physical or I can't work for you. I'm not investing my life in this only to find out in the middle of the campaign that you have some awful disease. And then if the disease is bad enough, I wouldn't even be able to yell at you, which would be very stressful for me."

"Fine. I'll get a physical."

"Right away."

"Fine."

Monty started walking again, kicking some pebbles as he did so, and Gorgoni walked alongside.

"Sorry about the medical stuff but I have to do my job correctly."

"I understand."

"At least you're a lefty. I noticed when you filled out your scorecard."

"What difference does that make?"

"Lefties tend to get elected president. They have trouble using scissors as children, develop a sense of injustice, and it feeds that fire in the belly that drives them to the White House."

"You may be oversimplifying."

"Reagan, the first Bush, Clinton, Obama. Harry Truman. Lots of lefties."

"Al Gore's a lefty, too."

"Yup. That's why it's pretty clear he was actually elected."

"Too bad they didn't bring that up before the Supreme Court."

Monty gave him a sideways glance.

"Any skeletons in your closet?"

"I can't swim."

"I wouldn't call that a skeleton. You're not running for life-guard. Why didn't you ever learn—?"

"My old man couldn't swim, and I didn't want to—it's embarrassing. It's like being illiterate; eventually you figure you're too old to learn and you avoid—"

"Any other skeletons? Maybe something more impressive?"

"Not that I know of." He thought hard. "I take a shitload of supplements."

"Yeah, I know. That's not a skeleton, either. What do you take?"

"Hawthorn, ginkgo, milk thistle, arjuna, cayenne…"

"You take cayenne?"

"Yeah."

"Does that work for what they say that works for?"

"I think so."

Monty nodded thoughtfully. "Good for you."

"Thanks."

"I'll need to meet with your family."

"Fine."

"How much do you take?"

"Of the cayenne? Four hundred fifty milligrams."

"And it really works?"

"Haven't had a problem."

"And you've been able to keep it in your pants?"

"Yes."

"So you'd recommend it?"

"What do you mean by recommend it?"

"As safe and effective."

"Haven't had a problem."

"If you have one of those four-hour incidents, you know, you're supposed to call your doctor."

"If I have one of those four-hour incidents, I'm calling a press conference."

"While we're on the subject, you'll need to bone up on foreign policy. Make sure you know the names of the leaders of thirty or forty of the top countries in the world, and get used to name-dropping those names."

"Anything else?"

"If you get a chance, you might want to learn how to swim. I don't want you drowning."

He had never before taken a cab all the way from Indianapolis to Bloomington, but this trip was full of firsts. This was also the first time he had ever flown home without alerting Caroline; she was expecting him to fly from Louisiana to Washington. He was enjoying the thought of surprising her. It had always been a solid marriage, he felt, as marriages go, but he considered it deficient in the spontaneity department. Rarely did they seem to do anything on a whim. Not that his current, hastily arranged trip was entirely whimsical, he reminded himself, since it did after all involve the presidency. He passed the time discussing politics with his cab driver, who had no idea who he was. The driver, a garrulous, unshaven Hungarian immigrant sporting a black beret, described himself as a libertarian; he believed that out-of-control government spending was destroying the country he had adopted and loved. The only politician about whom he had anything good to say was Ronald Reagan, whose visage he desperately wanted to see carved onto Mount Rushmore. When Gorgoni asked him who should pay for that, the conversation ended abruptly and the taxi appeared to speed up.

It was odd how energized he felt, all of a sudden. He had only just begun to enjoy the sense of relief attendant to his decision to not seek re-election to the House when the odd, unbidden cry had arisen that he should aim for the presidency. His first instinct had been to shun that cry as absurd, but now that he had a concept for the campaign taking shape in his mind, and the only campaign manager he considered equal to the task aboard, his fear of a national campaign had begun to melt away. In fact, the prospect was beginning to appeal to him. Unlike his seemingly constant, rather dull Congressional campaigns, this would be a once-in-a-lifetime hail-Mary pass. He would not suffer, as he normally did every other year, the burden of the expectation of victory. And, most of all, he would be liberated by his mission: to speak the truth as he saw it, without concern for political implications.

Gorgoni gave the driver a handsome tip when the cab pulled up in front of his home on Walnut Street. The driver opened the trunk and handed him his suitcase; he carried it instead of extending the handle and using the wheels. He felt like he had the strength and energy of a man half his age.

He opened the door with his key. Nicole, who had been practicing on the piano in the living room, lit up with surprise, and ran to give him a hug.

"Dad! I didn't know you were coming home!"

"Yeah. I came back for a meeting."

"What meeting?"

"The one we're going to have tonight. Is your mother still at work?"

"I guess."

"And where's Mandy?"

"Upstairs, but she's busy now."

Gorgoni gave her a quizzical look.

"Okay. I'm in the mood for hot chocolate. Shall we have some hot chocolate?"

"I can make it for us. You look tired, Dad."

"I don't feel tired."

She ran off to the kitchen. He carried his suitcase up the stairs to his bedroom. He resolved not to knock on Mandy's door if it was closed, as it proved to be.

At the living room piano, Nicole played for her father the song she had recently learned, *Candle in the Wind*, hitting only a couple of wrong notes. He applauded, and then they sat at the dining table where their steaming cups of hot chocolate awaited them.

"So what's this meeting about?" Nicole asked.

"Well, we should discuss it when we're all here," Gorgoni said.

"You're running for president, aren't you?"

"Can you keep a secret?"

"Definitely."

"If you want me to, and Mandy wants me to, and, most importantly, your mother wants me to, I'm going to do it. But I have to get everyone's approval."

"I would love to live at the White House. That would be like one of the coolest things I've ever done."

"I may not win, Nicole."

"That's the wrong attitude, Dad."

"No, that's the right attitude. If you attach yourself to winning, to living at the White House, to all the privileges that come with being part of the First Family, you'll only be disappointed. The prize isn't going to be winning. The prize will be in how we conduct the campaign. It's going to be different."

"Aren't you going to have rallies and speeches and bumper stickers like everyone else?"

"Yeah. But here's the difference. In those speeches, I'm going to omit all the usual bullcrap and I'm going to say what needs to be said to make sure you and your generation have a secure future."

"C'mon, Dad, that's impossible. The future is screwed up. The whole planet is burning up."

"Don't be pessimistic, it's unhealthy."

"I thought you wanted to tell the truth."

"It's my job to thread that needle. And it's your job now to be a good actress."

"Why?"

"Because when your mother gets here and we have the meeting, remember, you don't know anything. I want everyone to hear about it at the same time. Think you can pull that off?"

"So we're going to start this whole campaign of truth with a lie?"

"Life is full of contradictions. Play me some more Elton John, okay?"

As Nicole bounded to the piano, Gorgoni heard Frazier Milner say, "'Night, babe," and then saw the tall, awkward teenager make his way down the stairs. Frazier walked directly towards him, and Gorgoni stood to shake his hand. The boy had fair skin set off by a bright red pimple on the tip of his nose.

"Congressman, Frazier Milner, sir. Unofficially, I'm Mandy's boyfriend, but she's like, not down with the term, so we'll just say friends with favors, but don't sweat it, these are really small favors. They're more like token gestures. Her feelings for me aren't as intense as mine for her, but that's cool, I accept reality. You got to care enough not to care. You know what I mean?"

"Care enough not to care…"

"Right. Truly an honor to meet you, sir, and you can count on my vote."

And with that, Frazier turned and walked out of the house, as Nicole began playing *Can You Feel the Love Tonight*.

Caroline whipped up a dinner of corkscrew artichoke pasta with basil pesto, long a favorite of Gorgoni's, to celebrate his unexpected presence. In deference to her concern about how tired he looked, he napped on the den couch while she cooked. It took her under a half hour to prepare the pesto from fresh greens purchased at the farmer's market, while cooking an array of vegetables—zucchini, eggplant, tomatoes, and spinach—to top off the dish. Using wooden spoons, she stirred the boiling pasta with one hand and the vegetables in a sauté pan with the other. Finally, she garnished the bowls of corkscrews, vegetables, and pesto with sundried olives.

The smell of tomatoes and basil filled the dining room, and the family had never seemed more close-knit. Nicole sprinkled her bowl with soy parmesan and then passed the faux cheese to her sister. The two girls were now old enough that they could bond, instead of merely provoking one another. Caroline and Gorgoni each had a glass of pomegranate wine with the meal, while the girls drank spring water flavored with fresh mint leaves.

They talked about Mandy's science project, involving earthworms and topsoil depletion, and about Nicole's desire to learn to play alto sax. They talked about how much time Nicole was wasting on *Facebook*, and what to do about it. Even Nicole wasn't happy with *Facebook;* she was annoyed by the competition to have hundreds of friends, whether she really knew them or not. They talked about what colleges Mandy should apply to, and whether she should choose one or two "safe" schools. They talked about Frazier Milner; Gorgoni asked where he was applying and expressed relief that all of his favored colleges were different and some were far away. And they talked about Caroline's ambition that the family take a vacation to Brazil sometime in the next year.

When they finished their meal, Gorgoni took the empty bowls to the kitchen, then returned to announce that he wanted to have a family meeting in the living room.

"Oh, what's up?" Nicole said.

"I'll tell you in a moment," Gorgoni said, sitting on the green fabric loveseat, and putting his arm around Caroline as she sat down beside him.

"Is this why you came home?" Mandy said, sitting with her sister on the couch opposite.

"Yes," Gorgoni said.

"I think I know what this is about," Mandy said.

"I'm glad you do because I for one am totally in the dark," Nicole said. "What do you think it's about?"

"Let Dad tell us," Mandy said. "I don't want to steal his thunder."

He stroked his mustache. It wasn't his daughters' reaction that concerned him, but he could sense Caroline's spine stiffening already.

"Sometimes on the Floor, decisions can be made only by unanimous consent. This is one of those times. If everybody's on board, I'm going to run for president."

Before he could see Caroline's reaction, he could hear Nicole's.

"Wow! I don't believe it! Oh God, you're really going to run? That's unbelievable! This is so shocking, Dad, but it's what you and Mom always taught us—you have to believe in yourself. I support you, Dad. If I could vote, I'd definitely vote for you. Wow, this is amazing!"

Gorgoni turned to the daughter with the more nuanced approach to experience. "Mandy?"

"I'm in," she said. "But I want veto power over my Secret Service dudes."

"Me too," said Nicole.

Gorgoni turned to Caroline. "Honey, if you object, it's no go."

She ran a hand through his hair. "I'm dubious," she said.

"Why?"

"It'll be a strain on your health."

"I'll take Korean ginseng."

"Evan, you need rest. The demands of a national campaign are superhuman."

"Kicking myself for not running would also be a strain on my health."

"All the same…" Her voice trailed off.

"What is it?"

"Honey, I don't think you've been completely yourself lately. Not since the hospitalization."

"Maybe I'm completely myself now and I wasn't completely myself before."

"Passing out turned you into your true self? Is that what you're saying?"

"I'm not ruling it out. Stranger things have happened."

"When?"

"Look at Jack Abramoff. If ever there was a changed man—"

"Don't compare yourself to Jack Abramoff. You didn't go to prison."

"No, but I've done fifteen years in Congress. That's more time than he did."

She saw that he wasn't going to give ground on the question of whether he was physically and psychologically up to the challenge. She took his hand in hers.

"I thought you were done with politics."

"That's what I thought, too."

"What changed?"

"Suddenly there's the chance to actually make a difference. People seem to believe that I have something to offer the country. Even if it's only to make the case in Iowa and then close shop."

"The whole family will be put under a microscope."

"What do we have to hide?"

"Nothing to hide, but do we want our lives turned into a reality show?"

"I'm not worried." He turned to their daughters. "Are you worried?"

There was a chorus of "no" from the girls.

"You need a rationale for running," Caroline went on. "What's the rationale?"

Gorgoni had his answer at the quick. "Everyone else stinks."

"That's not good enough. It needs to be about your own vision."

He pondered the exigency for a long moment.

"*I can see*," he said at last, "that everyone else stinks."

Caroline shook her head. "Without a central vision—"

"Oh, come on," Gorgoni said, some irritation in his voice. "Is there no place for a candidate who's upfront about going into the thing blind as a bat?"

"That's his vision!" chimed in Mandy. "An America safe for candidates who are clueless! He's got over four million views on *YouTube* and it's mainly because he's, like, completely stumped by current events!"

"Totally," Nicole agreed.

"Mom, you know how you always say you have to take risks and go for it in life, even if you make mistakes?"

"Yes, but—"

"Well, if Dad doesn't run, I'm going to be so bummed, I'm going to go for it with Frazier."

Gorgoni raised his eyebrows and looked at Caroline with concern.

"That's it," she said. "We're running."

The assisted living facility in Salem, Indiana, was as clean as it was modest. His mother had been apprehensive about moving there some five years earlier, when she was eighty-five, but she had expressed no regrets since. She was a social person, and having outlived many of her friends, she took pleasure in making new ones. Many of those new friends at the facility were younger than she; a handful were older; but few had as much energy, and fewer still had the same clarity of mind. But as she always said, you need only a few good friends.

"I'm running for president, Mom," Gorgoni said. They were sitting in the facility's dining room, each table appointed with a bouquet of tulips, and had just been served a vegetable casserole.

"Well, you know I try to stay out of your business, but are you sure that's what you want?"

"I think I need to do it. We're in some peril as a country."

"Do you have any chance to win?"

"I'd have to be a fool not to be skeptical."

"So you're skeptical?"

"Yes."

"That's good. We can't afford a foolish president."

"Will you vote for me?"

"By absentee ballot. It's so much easier, dear."

"That's fine."

"If you get elected, I want you to increase Social Security benefits."

"That'll have to wait until I get the budget in order."

"Well, do whatever you have to do first but hurry up with it and don't forget what I told you."

"Right."

"It really isn't enough to live on, for most people. I'm lucky that you help me foot this bill."

"Right."

"I never thought you'd be president when you were a truck driver."

"Well, I'm still a long way from being president."

"Yes, but you're even further away from being a truck driver. Will the Teamsters get behind you?"

"They're committed to Oakley."

"He's a cheater."

"They really don't care about that, and maybe neither should you."

"Oh, I've voted for cheaters before. I liked Clinton. But I don't even see what the women see in Oakley, that's the difference. At least Clinton's a charmer."

"Right."

"You were never a natural charmer like that but I'm glad. I think that made you a better person. I hope it doesn't stand in your way as a candidate."

"Thanks, Mom."

"Make sure I get my absentee ballot. I'm not standing in line."

Dr. Solvang had been recommended by an old friend who had succeeded Gorgoni as principal at Bloomington High North and who had always voted for him, he said, to prevent him from reclaiming his former position. The doctor stood a trim six-two, had receding blond hair and wore rimless spectacles. He had an unassuming manner.

"Every pet I've owned has more medical history than you," Dr. Solvang said, taking Gorgoni's blood pressure.

"There's a side to me that's fatalistic."

"Is there also a side to you that isn't fatalistic?"

"No."

"Hundred five over seventy. That's nice and low."

"Sounds fine to me."

"Yeah. Healthfully low. Tell me, do you have a problem with doctors?"

"No, I like them very much as people. I just don't like to be around them when they're working. I have some cousins who are doctors. I think they were raised to be doctors from the crib."

"Yeah, a lot of my colleagues always knew they'd be doctors. Not me. I tried to be a concert pianist first. Couldn't make a living." Dr. Solvang put the blood pressure monitor aside and shone a light in Gorgoni's eyes, instructing him to look to one side, and then to the other. "And so you never go for check-ups?"

"Honestly, I'm not high on their usefulness."

"Uh-huh," Dr. Solvang said. "You've never had a colonoscopy, have you?"

"No."

"It's recommended for everyone over fifty."

"Mind if I wait till a hundred?"

"It can save your life. If there's a polyp—"

"I'll take my chances. I eat right."

"Of course, a good, balanced diet is crucial, but it doesn't mean you don't have any polyps. I strongly recommend a colonoscopy for any patient over fifty."

"Thanks, doc. I'll keep that in mind. I appreciate your concern."

"You don't take any medicines?"

"I take herbal supplements."

"There's no evidence that they work."

"That may well be true. I take them as insurance."

"Do you have medical insurance?"

It was evident that Dr. Solvang didn't know who he was, which was a good thing.

"Yeah, I get it through work."

Dr. Solvang completed the rest of the examination with hardly a word.

"Dad, if I get married, can we have the wedding in the Rose Garden?" Mandy said. She and her father were sitting on the front porch in the wicker rocking chairs that had been there since she was a little girl.

"Depends on who you marry," Gorgoni said.

Just then Monty pulled up in his black Volvo. Gorgoni stood up and waved.

"Who's that?" Mandy asked.

"That's our ticket," Gorgoni said.

"Monty?"

"Yup."

"What's so great about this guy?"

"He believes, on some level, that he's no more than a monkey, and that politicians are no more than dogs, and that gives him a unique perspective on politics."

Monty emerged from the car, his shirt tail hanging over one side of his sagging pants. He possessed a gait that recalled nothing so much as a penguin on speed.

Mandy pondered for a moment. "I can see why you're so high on him," she said.

⟨———⟩

Monty and the whole Gorgoni family sat around the dining table, where Caroline served a homemade cheese with homemade crackers.

"This is delicious," Monty said. "I never had cheese like this."

"Probably not," Caroline said.

"And these crackers are remarkably dry," Monty said.

"It's my own recipe. Garlic flaxseed crackers. They're dehydrated."

"Is that right?" Monty held up a cracker and inspected it. "Mm-hm. You know, these would be good to dunk in tea."

"Yes."

"Except they might soak up all the tea and leave the cup dry. Did Evan happen to have any of these the day he passed out?"

"I'm trying to decide where to make best use of Monty's diplomatic skills in my administration," Gorgoni said. "I'm thinking U.N. Ambassador."

"Thanks, but I can't possibly leave the track—"

"Those poor dogs," Caroline said.

"I can't leave it for eight years."

"You mean I have to serve two terms?" Gorgoni said, crestfallen.

"Let's see if you can make it past Iowa," Monty said.

"I had a check-up," Gorgoni said.

"What's the verdict?"

"Cholesterol of a hundred forty. Blood pressure, a hundred five over seventy. All my numbers were perfect. I'm healthy as a horse, apparently."

"Did you have a colonoscopy?"

"He didn't feel it was necessary in my case."

"Why not?"

"Because he did a prostate exam and he said that was good enough. The doc's an accomplished concert pianist, has remarkably long fingers."

"Then there's no reason not to run."

"How can the women of the family help?" Caroline asked.

Monty smiled at her with appreciation. "Three rules," he said. "One: don't say anything stupid. For the purposes of this campaign, your job is to be yourselves, be charming, but remain in the background. I hate to use the term wallpaper—"

"There goes the U.N. position," Gorgoni said.

"But if anyone's going to say anything stupid and blow the campaign, let it be the candidate," Monty said.

"Cool," Gorgoni said.

"Two: if you goof up and say something stupid, inform me immediately. Three: remember, just between us, we're not in this to win. We're in this to castigate the bastards. So don't be disappointed when we lose. It's all part of the plan."

"Whose plan?" Mandy said.

"We don't know that yet," Monty said. "Some believe there's a deity, others dispute that. I tend to be skeptical myself."

Nicole screwed up her face into a look of utter confusion. "So you're planning to lose?" she said, her voice dripping with disbelief.

"We're planning to let your father speak his mind," Monty said. "If I thought that was a foolproof recipe for success, I'd be naïve, and naïve people don't last long in the dog racing business. Any other questions?"

The Gorgoni women looked like they'd been stunned into silence. Gorgoni spoke up.

"Yeah, I've got a question," he said.

"Shoot," Monty said.

"Can we run this campaign with dignity? Can we do it without *Facebook*?"

"No."

"Aw, hell. You have no idea how many friends I'm going to have."

The crickets sounded festive, highlighting how otherwise still was Walnut Street on a humid July evening in Bloomington. Monty, Gorgoni, and Caroline sat in three of the four wicker rockers that had graced their porch for so long, the empty chair separating the candidate from his Svengali. The occasional vehicle passed by, always driven at a safe speed, and sometimes occupied by a driver or passenger who waved to the congressman and his wife. Gorgoni thought about how he missed these quiet summer evenings at home. He was having trouble concentrating on all his campaign manager's advice.

"The country's crying out for a cheap president," Monty was saying. "That means twelve dollar haircuts, meals in diners, overnight stays with supporters, and traveling by bus a lot. And this whole enterprise has to be funded by donations that cap out at twenty bucks. We refuse any donations over twenty bucks."

Caroline rocked herself forward in an instant and stayed there. "Twenty dollars! You're joking?"

"No."

"How in the world do you fund a national campaign on twenty dollar donations?"

"You get five million of them online."

"That's a hundred mil," Gorgoni said.

"That's impossible!" Caroline said.

"Getting that many contributions—that *is* daunting," Gorgoni said. "How about we top out at fifty bucks?"

Monty considered the suggestion, but only for a moment.

"If we go as high as fifty bucks, you may get corrupted."

Caroline made a loud scoffing sound that appeared to momentarily silence the crickets.

"Okay, twenty it is," Gorgoni said, stroking his mustache meditatively. "You really think we can get five million contributors?"

"We can, if we have Haroon Raj."

"Who's that?"

"Steve Jobs once offered him the moon to design for Apple. Haroon turned him down and moved to a farm in Colorado to grow Belgian endive. He's out of politics but he'll work for me. We once spent five days together at a sweat lodge in New Mexico where he gained enormous respect for my shamanic powers."

"You have shamanic powers?" Gorgoni asked.

"Only when I get sweaty," Monty said.

Caroline struggled to contain a degree of exasperation. "What exactly does an endive farmer have to do with raising a hundred million dollars?"

"Couple him with a good ad guy, and he'll hit so many eye-balls over the web—every day for this guy is like the Super Bowl. He'll raise Evan a fortune without anyone picking up a phone."

"Does he have a political bent?" Gorgoni said.

Monty shrugged. "Big supporter of endive subsidies, that's all I know."

Gorgoni and Monty agreed to try to enlist the help of Haroon Raj, and to hold off on hiring any more staff until the campaign contributions began to come in.

If any did.

CHAPTER TWO
The Primary

*T*he Jefferson-Jackson Dinner was the event for which the political class had been salivating for weeks. It was to be held on a Saturday night in November, the last weekend before Thanksgiving, in Des Moines' Hy-Vee Hall, a massive, modern downtown exhibition hall, highly prized by the locals. Monty had been at his wit's end for some time, trying to convince his candidate to prepare a speech. He had offered to hire a speechwriter. He had presented Gorgoni with an impressive list of speechwriters, authors, and retired journalists whom he claimed, with some bravado, he could engage at the drop of a hat—to no avail. He had offered to write the speech himself. He had even attempted to enlist Caroline, who didn't know whether or not to take him seriously, to withhold her favors until a speech was written. After one loud argument between the men over the matter in a hotel room at night—Caroline having nixed the idea of overnight stays with supporters, a suggestion of Monty's to save the campaign money—Nicole volunteered to write her father a speech, and Monty appeared so desperate that he paused for a moment before waving her away.

Gorgoni insisted as a point of pride that no speechwriter be engaged to put words in his mouth. He was confident that he would come up with something to say, if not this night, then the next, and if not the following, then certainly by Saturday night in Hy-Vee Hall. He was not overly concerned, and he was a little amused that Monty got so worked up about it. He said that having his family around him during the week would help him focus. And so, as they had done twice before, Nicole and Mandy took a bus trip along with their father's hometown supporters, from Bloomington to Des Moines, for several days of campaigning. They would not miss the Jefferson-Jackson Dinner, especially since their old man appeared determined to wing it.

Gorgoni arose early on Saturday morning and, *sans* entourage, walked down Locust Street to Cowles Commons, where he found the farmers market bustling. Locally raised eggs, beef, pork, and ham were abundant, as were holiday turkeys. Gorgoni enjoyed shaking hands, meeting people, asking the farmers about their businesses, probing the patrons of the market about how they would prefer to change the course of the nation, and suggesting to all that they were wise to support their local growers. He found it all very enjoyable, except for the smell that arose from the stalls of the vendors of cheese and various meats. People seemed pleasantly surprised to meet him devoid of entourage, and he explained that he couldn't keep sane if he were forced to remain within a candidate's bubble twenty-four hours a day. A vendor of butter and other dairy products asked him how he then intended to keep sane as president. Stumped, he conceded that the vendor made a very good point, and asked him in turn if he had any ideas for a speech he had to give that very night at the Jefferson-Jackson Dinner. The vendor also looked stumped.

Caroline chided him, upon his return to the hotel, for his disappearance, and he promised yet again to report on his whereabouts more responsibly. He deplored the loss of freedom that his candidacy imposed upon him, or at least was supposed to impose on him. He cut Caroline's chiding short, however, with a fine excuse: he had to think about what he would say tonight at the big dinner. He lay on his back in bed, fully clothed, hands clasped behind his head, and closed his eyes. Caroline left him alone in the room, and went out with the girls to shop for a new winter coat for Nicole. Caroline had long ago learned that shopping could serve a campaign well; there were lots of voters in stores, and the press coverage was always fluffy and positive.

That evening, in Hy-Vee Hall, the three presidential candidates—Gorgoni, Senator Nate Poston, and Senator Carl Oakley—were seated next to each other on one side of the stage, as Minority Leader Nina Paley, a well-coiffed woman of seventy-six, took center stage in a magenta pantsuit to an appreciative ovation. Gorgoni sat between his opponents, and greeted both of them warmly, although he detected some coolness in return from Poston, who apparently felt that Gorgoni had given him his word that he would not run, and whose aides had already anonymously elaborated upon that sense of betrayal to the press. Carl Oakley was dark-haired, forty-two, and only about five-foot-six, with a strong jaw and sculpted cheekbones; in his well-cut blue-grey suit with a thin black tie, he looked like a fashion model for the shorter man. Oakley was as gregarious as he was ambitious, and seemed to Gorgoni, if not a genuinely caring soul, at least a dependable warrior for the working class. His major complaint with Oakley, aside from the womanizing, was that the man did not seem to have a single original idea; he was an old-style union Democrat, his speeches reminiscent of those of icons of the past of his party, Hubert Humphrey and Tip O'Neill. Gorgoni felt that Oakley's time had come and gone.

Congresswoman Paley revved up the crowd with predictions of doom for the Republicans, and spoke glowingly of her party's agenda in that nation's capital, objectives that she swore could be reached only if the Democrats could regain a solid majority in both Houses. She knew as well as anyone that the electoral fate of the person at the head of the ticket would determine more than anything whether she would return to the House as Minority Leader or Speaker. She would not endorse, at least not early on, but it was never too early for her to focus on electability, and she used the word more than once in her opening remarks.

Having drawn the short straw, Senator Poston would speak first. Congresswoman Paley introduced him, with a knowing smile, as the next president of the United States. Poston, who had recently lost weight in preparation for his election sprint, looked a little haggard in a slightly baggy grey suit. Still, he rose with a confident nod to what he clearly felt was an accurate prediction of his immediate future.

As Poston began by expressing his heartfelt appreciation to Congresswoman Paley and, one-by-one, to Iowa's Democratic office-holders, the Chairwoman of the Iowa Democratic Party, several of the County Chairs, his own family of five, and finally the assembled guests, Gorgoni turned his thoughts to the speech he would have to shortly deliver. In the hotel room, he had noodled on the idea of tracing how life in America had changed since his childhood, trying to find in those changes a trajectory that might inform some inspired view of the future; in the end, though, he decided that that approach didn't lend itself well to improvisation, the only course left to him. He considered giving an uplifting speech about all the things that were best about America—baseball, high-tech innovation, the popular distaste for aristocracy, the eternal rooting for "the little guy," pre-school education, Social Security, the YMCA, public broadcasting, satellite radio, roasted chestnuts, small town libraries, dog parks, bicycle lanes, hiking trails—but as he began formulating the speech in his mind, he found himself humming Maria's *My Favorite Things* tune from *The Sound of Music*, and he took that as a warning. In the end, he decided to prepare nothing at all, and simply speak the truth as he saw it as the moment presented itself.

"...Then, finally, let us move forth and create, for once and for all, an America that is truly a shining city on a hill," Poston concluded, to rousing applause. Poston took his seat next to Gorgoni, who patted him on the back.

As Congresswoman Paley stepped up to the podium to introduce Oakley, too, as the next president of the United States, Gorgoni reflected on the strangeness of finding himself sitting on this stage. Maybe, after all, that was something he could talk about. He had never sought a career in politics. Truly. Many politicians claimed to have gotten into the game only from a humble calling to public service, but they were usually the most ambitious of the lot. No, Gorgoni hadn't been completely selfless in his desire to serve, and he wouldn't claim an absence of ego, but neither had he ever dreamed of embarking on this career until Caroline had rather persistently urged him on. More than most politicians, Gorgoni had stumbled into his political opportunities. Caroline had witnessed his popularity as principal of Bloomington High North and his own eagerness to help out their neighbor Lou Cullum when Lou ran, successfully, for State House. She kept saying that he was a political natural. When Lou decided after one term to run for State Senate, Lou and Caroline teamed up to persuade Gorgoni to take his shot at the State House seat. After two terms there, the Congressional seat opened up, and it seemed like half the Democratic officeholders in Indiana called upon Gorgoni, pleading with him to run. Caroline made the case that he had outgrown local politics and was ready for the big leagues, where he could really make a difference. A poll was commissioned that showed that he would win easily. It would have seemed irrational to turn away. Eight terms in the House of Representatives followed, and burned him out, and yet now here he was, about to be introduced at the seminal event leading up to the first-in-the-nation caucus in the presidential campaign, and wondering what the hell to say. There was a germ of an idea there, in the haphazardness of his own path, but he needed time to develop it, and Oakley was wrapping up.

"...We can again lead the world not only in military might but in social justice, in the decency with which we treat the sick and the old, and the greatness for which we prepare the young! Thank you, and God bless America!"

To Gorgoni's ears, Oakley received an even more rousing ovation than had Poston. The whole place was on its feet. Oakley was younger and better looking than Poston, and his suit fit. He was further to the left on many issues; clearly he had an appeal to the base of the party, though he couldn't raise funds on Poston's level. Gorgoni hadn't been able to listen to Oakley's speech since his mind was occupied knocking around ideas for his own, but he shook his hand and congratulated him on a fine speech.

Congresswoman Paley walked up to the mic again, applauding as she did so. She waited for the ovation to die down. "And now I give you the next president of the United States, Congressman Evan Gorgoni of Indiana!"

Gorgoni felt himself buoyed by the applause as he strode over to the podium and gave Leader Paley a handshake and a peck on the cheek. He felt light on his feet, as if he had just had three or four beers. It was a kick to have so many people giving him their utmost attention. He waved a couple of times, bowed his head slightly, and waited for silence. It took a while to come, and when it came, he let it last for an unusually long period of time, as he considered what to say. The crowd was entirely still, as he was, and then there came a kind of collective sigh, a susurration tinged with laughter, and then there was stillness again. He saw the audience at first as a single, giant mass, and then he allowed himself to focus on a single table, not far from the stage, where Caroline and his daughters and Monty sat. He couldn't help but smile when he saw Monty lower his head.

"Thank you, Iowa. *Caucus* is a Native American term. It means a meeting of tribal leaders. And I say to you, tribal leaders, let's be realistic. There ain't no shining city on a hill." He heard some stirring in the crowd, and a few hands clapping. "There's just the decaying cities we've got and their roads that need to be paved and bridges that need to be maintained. How about if we simply try to do our best? Without the grandiose promises. How about if for once we confront our challenges with a grounding in the truth? Can we trust the Republicans or even the Democrats? Probably not. Can we bridge our differences and begin a more civilized discourse? Probably not. Can we at least agree as a society to put our children first, to create an educational system second to none, so all our children can meet their potential? Probably not. Can we create a health care system that is affordable and efficient and humane? Probably not. Can we construct a nationwide network of bullet trains? Probably not."

And now a chant rose from the crowd, tentatively at first, beginning in the back of the hall and working its way forward.

"Probably not! Probably not!"

Gorgoni went on. "Can we stop the fearsome onslaught of climate change, the melting of the glaciers and the droughts and floods and storms brought on by more energy in the atmosphere? Probably not."

"Probably not! Probably not!" the crowd chimed in.

"Can we put an end to our dangerous dependence on fossil fuels that threatens the planet and enriches unstable regimes?"

"Probably not!" The answer echoed in the hall.

"Can we find the political will to insist that clean sources of energy fuel the lion's share of our economy? Probably not. Can we fund our entitlements? Probably not. Can we get our budget in balance? Probably not."

"Probably not! Probably not!" roared the crowd. Gorgoni gazed across the hall, and saw a sea of smiles and nodding heads and waving arms and some people even jumping up and down with something like relief.

He imbibed the energy of the crowd and pressed on, his cadence rhythmic, his volume rising, the whole force of his being merging with his audience. The microphone had become redundant.

"Can we beat our swords into plowshares and make war no more? Probably not. Can we at least stop crime right here at home? Probably not. Can we get our justice system to actually dispense justice, and to do so with compassion and decency? Probably not. Can we make this a more perfect Union? Probably not. Can we rise up as a nation and say, *this is our land, our people, our government*—and we will take it back to protect the weakest and most helpless among us—take it back from the moneyed and the privileged, the special interests and their lobbyists? Probably not. Do we have to try, anyway? Do we have to try, anyway?"

There was silence in the hall.

"Do we have to try, anyway? That's the question. Thank you, Iowa!"

The audience jumped to its feet almost as one, its applause deafening. Gorgoni waved and beamed. He felt confirmed in his judgment that there was really little point in preparing these speeches. He glanced over at the other two candidates, who managed to smile at him through self-evident fear. Out in the crowd, he saw Caroline standing, shaking her head slightly in amazement, a concerned look on her face; next to her, Monty raised his head and lifted himself up ever-so-slowly, wearing the expression of a man who had been thrown off a sea cliff and landed on a raft.

The momentum that began at the Jefferson-Jackson Dinner did not abate during the days that followed. Monty kept relaying better and better news about campaign contributions and sanguine web-view reports from Haroon Raj, to whom Gorgoni had never spoken; the man apparently refused contact with actual candidates. The crowds at the coffee klatches and town halls set up by the campaign's hip young advance team headed by Hannah Svoboda, a young, slight woman with two diamond studs in her nose who looked like the heroine of a Stieg Larsson novel, could not have been more encouraging. After an exhausting four-day swing through Iowa, Caroline and Gorgoni sat on the bed in their Holiday Inn room somewhere in Pocahontas County, nibbling on trail mix, and watching Chris Matthews sum up the early status of the race. Gorgoni wore an old pair of blue-striped pajamas, while Caroline was in a pastel green nightgown and had a white clay mask over her face.

"...And then there's Congressman Evan Gorgoni, the Hoosier phenomenon, whose web-based campaign is raking in the bucks. Is this guy onto something profound, or is he the Voice of Doom? When he speaks, I get a warm feeling down my legs, both my legs, and I'll be honest with you, I don't know if it's the fresh, honest, plain-spoken humanity in his voice or if I've just pissed myself. I really don't know."

Gorgoni muted Chris Matthews. "I can't believe three million came in overnight," he said.

"Haroon is worth his weight in gold," Caroline said.

"Today I met this kid who's been having nightmares since coming home from Iraq. Can't get a job. Living in his car. He comes over to me in the parking lot of the Rotary Club after my talk, and says thank you. What the hell is he thanking me for?"

"You're down by only three in the latest Rasmussen poll. In spite of Chris Matthews' new nickname for you. Which is catching on."

"I am not the Voice of Doom. I don't see myself as being about doom at all."

"You don't offer a ton of hope."

"That's because they're not reading between the lines."

"Uh-huh."

"They don't know what it means to go for the thing that—"

"If you say another word about singing, ever, I will blow the whistle on this campaign! End of story!"

Caroline's outburst left Gorgoni feeling as flustered as he was chastened. It was starting to gnaw at him that Caroline showed less enthusiasm for this campaign than she had shown for his countless campaigns for his ineffectual House seat.

"Who would you vote for, honestly?" he asked. "If you weren't constrained by marriage."

"Oakley," Caroline said. She got up from the bed and headed for the bathroom.

Gorgoni tailgated her right to the sink. "You would? He's a womanizer."

Caroline shrugged. "He's divorced." She squeezed some toothpaste out of the tube, onto her brush.

"So if a guy is married and cheats on his wife, that's bad? But then it's okay again if he gets divorced?"

"Why are we talking about this?" Caroline managed to say, through a mouthful of foam.

"Because I'd like to know that you're a hundred percent behind me."

Caroline kept brushing her teeth.

Later that evening, Gorgoni let his goodnight kiss to Caroline linger, and, employing techniques honed over two decades of marriage, initiated lovemaking. As Caroline began moaning with pleasure, close to orgasm, Gorgoni whispered into her ear.

"Caroline, I'm asking for your vote."

"That's not entirely fair," Caroline said.

The next morning, Monty drove Gorgoni to a local news studio where he could be interviewed remotely by Christiane Amanpour.

"Don't say anything negative about your opponents," Monty said.

"Of course not," Gorgoni said.

"She's going to egg you on."

"That's fine. The woman's got to do her job."

In the studio, Gorgoni was seated in front of a screen on which, after a few moments, Christiane Amanpour appeared. She greeted him politely and then cut to the chase.

"Congressman, if you become president, how would you create jobs?"

"We start by looking at what needs to be done. We have bridges and ports that need repair, toxic waste sites that need to be cleaned up, urban areas that need to be made safer and more livable, energy grids that need modernization. We could turn first to private industry, since we have a capitalist economy, and we could say, 'Is anyone out there planning to take care of these problems?' The answer will be no—since most businesses aren't in the business, for example, of repairing bridges from sheer good will. That's when government has to step in, partnering with private industry in a fair bidding process, to fix what needs fixing."

"But can we afford more government spending? What about the deficit?"

"We'll save a lot of money by getting our troops out of Germany and Japan, where, I would like to note, the war that sent them there is over. And we can cut the cost of Medicare in half. That'll give us plenty of money to get started with."

"Cut Medicare costs in half? How do you do that?"

"Eat healthier food."

"Excuse me?"

"Eat healthier food."

"To reduce medical costs?"

"Of course. I know, it's so obvious that I feel kind of stupid saying it."

"Why do you feel that your economic program is superior to that of Senator Poston or Senator Oakley?"

"They are both very nice fellows and upstanding gentlemen."

"But how do you feel about their economic programs?"

"I'm sure they've got terrific ones. Forgive me, but I've been concentrating on my own."

"But is your plan superior to your opponents'? And why?"

"My father taught me as a boy that it's not nice to say that what you have is better than what someone else has. I'd like to be president, but not if it means I have to be rude."

"Let's turn to our financial system itself. Congressman, you've been a critic of Wall Street and what you call 'high roller bankers.' What would you do specifically to fix the banking system?"

"I'd give a national test on economics to sixth graders around the country. The top five scorers serve on a banking oversight commission. Every year, before the banks can bring any new products to market—any new derivatives, or collateralized debt obligations, or credit default swaps—the CEOs of the banks have to explain those products to the panel of smart sixth graders. And if the sixth graders don't understand it, the banks don't get to sell it."

Gorgoni grabbed a lunch with Monty in a classy café in downtown Davenport. Gorgoni ordered a pasta primavera that he initially sent back to the kitchen because it came with cheese. Monty ordered baked salmon with Greek potatoes.

"You don't like cheese?" Monty asked.

"I don't remember cheese," Gorgoni said.

"When was the last time you had cheese?"

"The night before I got married."

"So this has something to do with Caroline?"

"Everything about me has something to do with Caroline. Even my children."

"And Caroline doesn't like cheese?"

"I think that's safe to say."

"Wait a minute. Didn't she serve me cheese in Bloomington?"

"That was made from nuts."

"Not real cheese?"

"She would never serve real cheese."

"Well, she doesn't have to like cheese, but it's better if nobody knows about it."

"The important thing is that she likes me."

"True."

"Maybe not to the point of voting for me, but she's definitely fond of me." Monty looked at him funny. "Where do we go next?" he asked.

"Coffee klatch. Bettendorf."

"Let's pick up Caroline at the hotel first."

"Right."

"Do I have to drink coffee?"

"No."

"Good."

"Oakley and Poston have new ads out today."

"Taking shots at each other again?"

"Yup. And we float above the fray."

"When are we going on the air with a spot?"

"Never. We just stay on the web. We're getting great press about not running ads, why fuck with it?"

It was a modest home in Bettendorf that looked to have been built in the fifties, with a large windowed area cut into sixteen square panes looking out from the living room to the street. A few dozen of the curious had gathered to hear the candidate. Gorgoni stood in the middle of a staircase that led up to the dining room, and addressed the voters in the living room.

"So far I've been able to campaign without making false promises. I can't promise how long that will last, but I intend to keep it going as long as I can. But I do feel that I can say this with a good deal of confidence: if I'm elected, we'll probably manage to muddle along. I'll take questions now."

A young woman of about twenty, with blonde hair down to her waist, and skin as pale as the inside of a radish, spoke up with fervor in her reedy voice.

"Congressman, I was canvassing for you, and an old woman said, 'Why should I vote for a guy who says he can't solve anything?' So many old people are naïve, and seem to believe in magic solutions to all our problems. How do we explain to them that they're running from reality?"

A couple of other young people in the room applauded.

"You should listen to your elders, respect them," Gorgoni said. "But, win or lose, it isn't in me to promise what I can't deliver. When you go to your caucus site on Tuesday, I want you to think about the promises the other candidates have made, and my lack of promises, and ask yourself, do I want one of the guys who's confident he can turn this country around on a dime, or do I want the guy who isn't so confident, and therefore will be asking questions and making objective analyses every step of the way? Evaluate that by whatever measure you choose."

An elderly woman spoke up, seated on a black leather couch under a painting of three brown horses running right at the viewer. Some of the people standing in the line of sight between her and Gorgoni moved aside.

"I want to say, I gave up on my dreams long ago and your hopelessness is refreshing. It makes me feel better about facing my own mortality."

"Thank you," Gorgoni said. "Mortality is nearly as tough to tackle as the deficit."

A middle-aged man said, "What are you going to do about the drug problem?"

Gorgoni stroked his mustache and nodded his head. "It's very serious. Americans have been spending way too much money in pharmacies."

"I meant illegal drugs," the man said.

"Oh, that's the cart dragging the horse," Gorgoni said. "If we're going to break the drug habit, first we have to reduce our appetite for legal drugs."

A dowdy woman in a grey turtleneck raised her hand. Gorgoni pointed to her.

"Do you have a strategy to prevent crime?" she wanted to know.

"Nip it in the bud," Gorgoni said. "Teach kids the difference between right and wrong in the first grade. Why has that never been in the curriculum?"

A woman in her fifties, dressed in a suit, asked her question in the pointed tone of a journalist.

"Will you drop out if you lose in Iowa?"

Gorgoni pondered the question, which took him by surprise.

"That's an idea," he said. "Thank you."

"Can anything be done to restore civility to politics in this country?" The booming voice belonged, oddly enough, to a small, plump man in a flesh-colored suit sporting wide lapels.

"We have to become to what the Lakota call *cante ohitika*—brave-hearted. Let the other side attack. If we're going to ensure the future of Mother Earth, we can't be distracted. We have to care enough not to care."

For a moment, nobody's hand went up. Then an obese woman right in front of the staircase raised hers, and Gorgoni nodded at her.

"I have heart disease. My cardiologist is recommending a bypass operation, but my HMO doesn't want to pay. They say the operation isn't necessary."

"I know something about heart disease. I lost my father to sudden cardiac arrest when he was forty-two and I was nine. He was the picture of health. After he died, my mother got a job in the town library, where she read every book on nutrition and heart disease that she could find. And so we began eating differently in our home. Here's what I'd recommend," Gorgoni said. "Stop eating everything you've been eating that's high in fat. Consume foods fresh from the farm that are colorful—red and green and yellow. Purple is good, too—eggplant, cabbage. The colors protect your heart."

"But what about the HMO that won't pay for my operation?" the woman asked, looking confused.

"Well, if you protect your heart with these vegetables, you may wind up thanking the HMO for their cheapness."

A burly man with a goatee cleared his throat.

"How do you feel about gay marriage?"

There was little disagreement, these days, on the Democratic side on this issue, so the subject didn't come up as often among

Democrats as among Republicans; Gorgoni rarely met a Democrat who stood in opposition.

"There are too many people on the planet," Gorgoni said, matter-of-factly. "We may need to encourage it."

In the rear stood a powerfully built man in his thirties with tattoos visible on his neck and his arms. The sleeves of his brown sweatshirt were rolled up, and his Pittsburgh Pirates baseball cap sat askew on what appeared to be a head shaved bare. There were silver rings on all ten of his fingers. He had tan skin, with thin lips and deep-set brown eyes that seemed devoid of life. His speech was halting and intense.

"What's your...position...on...assault weapons?"

Gorgoni smiled. "In my opinion, an insane way to go deer hunting, but that's just me."

A few people tittered, and the Pirates fan sneered.

Now a very angry man spoke up. He was not old, but had white hair that stood out against his red visage. There was a purplish tint to his broad nose. He offered more of a rant than a question.

"Our government consists of puppets who are owned lock, stock, and barrel by the banks and the multi-nationals, and I wonder if you're nothing more than the next puppet! You've been in Congress with the rest of 'em, schmoozed with the same lobbyists—you're another Washington insider! Why should I be stupid enough to believe you'd be anything different?"

There was some jeering from the gathering. The harsh tone and cynicism of the questioner appeared to offend the sensibility of the generally polite Iowan crowd.

"No, hey, it's a legitimate question," Gorgoni said, gesturing for quiet. "Will some industry pit its coffers against me and reduce my spine to jelly? I don't think so. Here's why. My wife owns me heart and soul. I remember now how scary it was when that happened—almost twenty-three years ago. So that door is shut. I made a commitment to Caroline; she owns me, no one else. Simple as that."

There were some "Awwws" from the crowd. Virtually everyone turned to Caroline, who was standing near the base of the staircase, and smiled or clapped lightly. Caroline looked up at her husband with a kind of sadness, and spoke in a tone of acquiescence.

"All right," she said. "I'll vote for you."

In the street, outside the home of the coffee klatch, Gorgoni noticed the man in the Pirates baseball cap staring at him before climbing into his pick-up truck. Inside the truck, the man started the engine, backed up, and then lurched the vehicle forward onto the street with tires screeching. He was listening to a bombastic voice on the radio.

"Not since Hitler," said the bombastic voice, "has a man as power-hungry and dangerous as Evan Gorgoni come forth to attempt to destroy everything that is good and decent and right and just. I say that with absolute certainty. I feel it, I know it, I sense it in every bone of my body. Not since Hitler!"

"We appear to have an upset in the making," the suave anchor-man was saying on the KCCI station, Channel 8, *First in Iowa News*. "Maverick Congressman Evan Gorgoni of Indiana, funded by over a million donations of twenty dollars each, leads with forty-seven percent of the vote. On the Republican side, Virginia Governor Malcolm Benneton has blown away the field…"

On the screen of the television in the hotel suite, Gorgoni, Monty, Caroline, and Mandy watched with quiet confidence, as Nicole jumped up and down, exclaiming, "I can't believe Dad's going to be president! I told you that you should run! Wow! I've changed the course of American history! That is so cool!"

"I said he should run, too," Mandy said.

"That's true," Nicole said. "You are absolutely a footnote to history."

"Let's see what Matthews is saying," Monty said, grabbing the remote and changing the channel to MSNBC.

Chris Matthews was sitting across the desk from pundit Norman Ornstein.

"This is stunning," Chris Matthews said. "Breathtaking! A stealth campaign that put no money, zilch, into TV ads, into traditional media, but poured it into the web, where clips of the candidate waxing metaphysical are ubiquitous. Is the Voice of Doom destined for greatness? Will we elect our first cosmic-American president? And is he stable enough for the job? Is the guy *off the rez*, or what? Norman Ornstein, you're as astute as any political prognosticator I know. Let me ask you this, sir: have you ever seen an upset like this? What is in the political ether? Is your underwear as damp as mine?"

Just as Norman Ornstein opened his mouth, the hotel room phone rang. Monty muted the set and answered the phone.

"Yeah? All right, I'll put him on the line, and you go ahead and tie in the senator."

Monty covered the mouthpiece and informed Gorgoni that Senator Poston was calling to concede. Gorgoni changed places with Monty on the couch and took the phone.

"Hello?" Gorgoni said. "Okay, I'll wait."

A moment later, Poston was on the line.

"Evan, congratulations, you son of a bitch," Poston said. "You whupped my ass."

"Sorry, Nate," Gorgoni said. "It was nothing personal."

"First you tell me you're not going to run, then you whup my ass."

"Sorry, Nate. I didn't do it on purpose. I had no idea it was going to happen."

"I wish I understood how the hell you did it."

"So do I."

"I'm going to make my concession speech now, then Carl's going to make his, then the night's yours."

"Thank you."

"I'll be as gracious as I can, even if you did play me for a sucker. I still like you and I'll always like you and something tells me I'm going to want you in my Cabinet. I'll see you in New Hampshire, friend."

"Hey, Nate, you got any advice for me in New Hampshire? You know the place like the back of your hand."

There was no response for a long moment.

"Why would I give you advice?"

"Oh, yeah. Sorry, I got carried away by the spirit of comity."

"Let's not take it too far."

"Right."

"Be well, Evan."

"Onward and forward, Nate."

Gorgoni hung up the phone, miffed that he had missed Norman Ornstein's response to the underwear question.

At the victory celebration in his Des Moines headquarters, Gorgoni attempted to quiet the crowd that greeted him with a roaring ovation.

"Thank you, my friends. Thank you, thank you, thank you, that's enough now. Calm down. I have spoken with Senator Poston and Senator Oakley, who have graciously conceded defeat. But defeat is an illusion as much as victory is; this is not a sport we're engaged in; it's more akin to poetry; it's all about the next word and who gets to say it. The people of Iowa have now had the last word. And they have said no to the politics of the past, and yes to the chance to embrace the future humbly, with an understanding of uncertainty, with a commitment to our brothers and sisters, with respect for the limitations of our species, and with a love of the land and the sea and the sky.

"We do not have all the answers, nor do we promise profound advances in all phases of everyday life. But we can pledge to at least consider the planet when we make decisions. We can permit ourselves to contemplate the benefits of peace, should it come, beyond even the saving of life and treasure. And we can stop insulting the intelligence of all Americans with simplistic ideologies. Government is not the solution, and it is not the problem. Government is the thing that collects taxes and paves roads and chooses to either invest or not invest in the future. Government is the thing that starts wars and sometimes can actually stop them. Government is the thing that provides a framework of laws that lifts our species up a few notches from life in the jungle. Government is the thing that gets corrupted despite its best intentions, and it is the thing that gets redeemed despite its worst excesses. Government is the thing that serves as the collective expression of our free souls, and that task, as we know, grows exponentially more messy with each new soul born into our territory, the territory of a nation bound by its celebration of freedom and justice.

"But most crucially, government is a thing. It is a thing. It is not a person. There's no point in hating it. It is a thing. I promise, if elected, to keep it a thing. And I will seek to advance, if I can—and I'm not promising that I can—but if I can, I will seek to advance the thingness of government by making it even more of a thing on the day I leave office than it was on the day I was sworn in. Maybe government will be bigger or maybe it will be smaller, but the thingness of government will be unquestioned. Everyone will know that government is a thing, merely a thing, and that should take some of the poison out of our democracy. Thank you for your support, and it's on to New Hampshire!"

The farmhouse in Western Pennsylvania was built on top of a small hill that looked out on land otherwise flat as far as the eye could see. The house was made of brick. Several salt-and-pepper asphalt shingles were missing from the roof. The front of the house had but one large window, with shutters painted green, and a small confederate flag suspended beside it. A grey metallic chimney rose from the roof. A couple of dozen vehicles, including quite a few pick-up trucks, Jeeps, and SUVs, were parked in a circular dirt driveway and on the grass alongside.

Inside the house, in an ample living room, a meeting was taking place. About sixty people were present, which was certainly all the room could hold. Some were standing, others were seated on folding chairs, and six women sat on an L-shaped sectional leather couch that was the room's central furnishing. Two men sat on the arms of the couch.

"Clinton and Obama were patriots compared to this guy," the speaker was saying. He wore a Pittsburgh Pirates baseball cap and his neck was tattooed with figures of mermaids. He stood on an ottoman and rapped his fingers, all adorned with silver rings, against the frame of a painting of the Madonna and child. "Gorgoni threatens everything that makes America *America*, even our right to have children."

A woman who stood barely over five feet tall, yet who must have weighed over two hundred pounds, chimed in from a corner of the room.

"He's a U.N. flunky! He's got to be exposed!"

"No! Not yet!" cried a self-assured young man with shaggy eyebrows and a long, coarse beard that made him look middle-aged. He tugged on his suspenders. "If we stop him now, then the Dems will still have a chance to nominate someone who can win."

The Pirates fan nodded his head. "You're right. Let them fucking implode. We hold our fire until he gets the nomination. He'll be a lot easier to beat than Poston. Hell, in the states with open primaries, let's turn out our people to hold their noses and vote for the son of a bitch."

Gorgoni stood on the stage at Moore Theatre on the Dartmouth campus and looked out upon the sea of young faces. They seemed younger than the students with whom he had attended Indiana University, and fatter, and straighter. They took for granted all manner of technologies that were unimaginable when he had attended university. And he knew by now, from countless conversations with young people in Iowa and from earlier campaign events on college campuses here in New Hampshire, that they had matured into an adulthood marked by cynicism: they had no faith in government, no confidence in their own economic future, little hope that the crisis that loomed in the nexus of energy, environment, and climate could ever be resolved. Many of them expected that, upon graduating into a sea of debt, they would need to move back home with their parents for an indefinite period of time. They had accepted gloom into the core of their beings much the way a person missing a leg learns to accept the loss, and they had moved on with their lives. In hotel lobbies late at night, Gorgoni had discussed often with Monty his impressions of what he had come to call the Deflated Generation; each time, Monty grew more and more excited. "These kids are perfect for you!" he would exclaim.

Gorgoni wanted nothing more than to give them some hope. But he would not do it with bromides.

"Let me begin with a story," he said. "When I was a boy of nine, my father took me to a big city, Chicago, for the first time in my life. He was a big, strapping, vigorous man; he would die of sudden cardiac arrest three weeks later. We stood on the shore of Lake Michigan, and I stared in awe at the skyline of the city that made my heart sing. I said, 'Pop, you think I'll conquer that city one day?' He didn't respond. So I went on, 'Well, is Mom right? When I grow up, can I be whatever I want to be?' He paused, smiled down at me, and said, 'Probably not.' That, I understand now, was his gift to me. That was his challenge. That, my friends, is why we stand here today. Facing reality with a cold eye does not spell defeat; it spells our only chance for triumph."

The applause was rousing, nearly deafening. Many of the students jumped to their feet; others stomped on the ground. In the back of the hall, Monty sidled over to Alvin Vernard, seventy, the elegant African-American power broker who ranked as the *éminence grise* of the Civil Rights movement. He was arguably the most respected political thinker on the left. "Alvin, how long are you going to stay on the sidelines?" Monty asked. "This thing's snowballing. Haroon is bringing in over a million a day without breaking a sweat."

Alvin Vernard just smiled.

Gorgoni was enjoying the scenic ride from Hanover to Dover along I-89, the traffic light and the unfolding views of forests and creeks and railroad tracks familiar and comforting. New Hampshire was one state that had found magic in slowing down the rate of change in daily life; Monty seemed to acknowledge the fact by driving more slowly than usual. The drives between campaign events were Gorgoni's only down time, save for his nights in hotels. He could clear his mind on a route like this. Even Hannah Svoboda seemed to have mellowed her approach to advancing events to accommodate the inclinations of the locals. There would be nothing frantic about this campaign.

"You think I should start writing my speeches in advance?" he asked.

"Nothing to lose by trying," Monty said.

"It doesn't appeal to me, though. Being scripted."

"Then don't."

"Anyone can get elected president. But to get elected while winging it the whole way, that's going for the thing that—hey, put that away!" Monty had taken his Blackberry out of his pocket and was reading a message while driving. "Don't ever do that again."

"Sorry. But you might want to know, Oakley's team is reaching out."

"What do they want?"

"The vice presidency, probably. They're hinting he'd be willing to endorse you in Manchester next week."

"I don't need him."

"They've got an impressive organization in New Hampshire. They've been running for a year. But they can read the polls."

"No deals. But if he wants to endorse, I accept gratefully. And ask him if he can send in twenty bucks."

He lay in his clothes atop the maroon bedspread pulled tight around a bed he had found, last night, a little lumpy. He was coming to hate hotel rooms. They militated against all that was best in his intentions. He wasn't sure why, but it was hard for him to read in a sterile room, hard not to turn on the television, hard to have an original thought. He could almost feel his brain atrophy in a rented room. Spending more than two or three waking hours in a hotel room was deadly to him, yet it was impossible to avoid on the campaign trail. He was beginning to consider it a national tragedy that hotel rooms were the breeding grounds of presidents.

On the television screen now was a local reporter, a young woman with an intense manner and wide eyes, looking cold in her overcoat as she spoke directly to camera with Senator Poston visible behind her, shaking hands at a factory gate.

"Fighting for his political life in his home state, Senator Poston knows that if he loses in New Hampshire, it's all over. He's taking nothing for granted, though he's leading in the polls by thirty points over the web-based insurgency of Congressman Evan Gorgoni."

Caroline emerged from the bathroom topless, grabbed the remote and shut off the television.

"How do we know that Oakley isn't talking to Poston, too?" she wondered.

"They hate each other. Poston suspects that Carl actually means what he says. In Poston's universe, that sort of thing is unforgivable."

"It wouldn't be a bad team, you and Carl. You complement each other."

"How?"

"He's upbeat. He's a can-do kind of guy."

"I know. It makes me uncomfortable."

Caroline sat down on the bed. Gorgoni sat up and massaged her neck.

"When you asked me to marry you, you didn't say, 'We'll muddle through.' You said, 'We'll have a beautiful life together.'" She looked at him pleadingly. He felt sad for her. Was she still in love with who he used to be?

"And haven't we…?"

"Yes."

"Hell, you may even become First Lady," he pointed out.

"I'm saying, you won me with optimism."

"Ah."

"You see?"

He pondered for a while. He was touched by her nostalgia for a simpler time, for that surely was what it was. He rose and looked out the window, where hotel guests ambled in a courtyard.

"Love clouds the mind," he said.

Monty chomped down on a poppy seed bagel as he sat in the Nashua campaign office and watched news coverage on a sixteen-inch television set that looked at least twenty years old. When delight invaded Monty's features, there was never anything remotely subtle about the phenomenon. His open mouth was a silent laugh; his eyes glowed with satisfaction. Kalani Graynight, the young press spokesman he had recently hired, leaned his long, slim frame against Monty's desk and watched the news with a poker face.

"Senator Poston set off a firestorm of controversy with his remark that the gun lobby has a quote '*stranglehold* on American politics,' and attempted to walk back his comments this morning," the reporter said. It was the same young woman in the same overcoat.

Now there followed footage of Senator Poston in front of a train station, shaking hands with commuters, and looking peeved to be asked a question about the *stranglehold* comment.

"Since when is *stranglehold* a dirty word?" he said. "I believe in the Second Amendment and I admire how the gun lobby has strangled, or I should say structured, the debate on firearms. Sometimes too much uninformed discussion can be a bad thing."

"It is for you, pal," Monty said, and turned off the television.

"He's still scared of the gun lobby," Kalani said.

"Apparently."

"That's pathetic."

"He's making the case for *strangleholds*. There's an upside to *strangleholds!* Wow! I told you he was too stupid for national politics. The only thing this fool has going for him is that he's the frontrunner. And you know when the worst time to be a frontrunner is?"

"When?" Kalani asked, dutifully.

"Before the first primary. It's an unearned title. People resent that. And they get to express their resentment on Election Day."

⟵⟶

The debate took place in the auditorium of Southern New Hampshire University in Manchester. The two hundred-odd seats were filled by a mix of students, faculty, and supporters of the three candidates, and five video cameras recorded the event from every conceivable angle. A middle-aged female moderator, a political reporter from the *New Hampshire Union Leader*, posed the questions. Oakley, Poston, and Gorgoni stood behind podiums about ten feet apart on the stage, Poston in the center. Oakley was attacking a question about education with the fast-paced, passionate, high-energy dynamism that defined his candidacy, when a red light flashed in front of him.

"…We have classes right here in Manchester with forty children—that shouldn't happen in America! It's an outrage! I want all American children—"

"Time," the moderator said.

"…to have the chance I had, to go to the best schools and have the individual attention—"

"Your time," the moderator said.

"…the attention they need. You need teachers, you need guidance counselors, you need principals and you need parents and they all have to work together. It does take a village. I want all American children to have the finest education in the world, and we can do that, I know in my gut we can do that, if we begin by putting our children first!"

"Senator Poston, same question, and I'll ask you again to please try to observe the agreed-upon time limits. How do we raise children's test scores?"

"With comprehensive educational reform," Poston said, in a clipped, assured tone. "This shouldn't be partisan. It's got nothing to do with ideology, it's about what works. If an idea works, I'm for it. If it doesn't, I'm against it. It's that simple. I can bring Republicans and Democrats together, taking the best ideas from both parties, and together, with a little common sense, we can get this done for the American people. And we must do it; it's a national necessity. We must give the appropriate level of resources to prepare the next generation for the challenges they will surely face. That will be a priority of my administration, the very highest priority. Our children come first. You can't be a nay-sayer when it comes to our children's future. You can't set limits on our children's dreams."

Poston turned now to Gorgoni, who stood to his right, pointed at him, and shook his head in dismay.

"My opponent here seems to base his whole campaign on limiting our hopes and expectations."

The red light flashed. "Time," the moderator said.

"Well, you can't do that in this country," Poston went on. "You can't limit hopes and dreams, it's not—"

"Time," the moderator said.

"It's not right. It defies the best in our character. It's a defeatist approach!" Poston said.

"Thank you, your time is up," the moderator said.

"We are not a nation of defeatists!" Poston put in.

The moderator turned to Gorgoni. "Congressman, you've just been called a defeatist. Under the rules of the debate, you have the right to respond. Do you care to?"

"No."

There was applause.

"Okay, then, Congressman Gorgoni, same question to you: how do we raise children's test scores?"

"Ask them easier questions," Gorgoni said. "I waive the balance of my time."

A hush overtook the room, and then a few snickers were audible.

"Could you explain what you mean by 'ask easier questions?'" said the moderator.

"Sure. Ask kids questions about how to download music for free on their cellphones—their scores will be off the charts. They'll all go to Harvard. But maybe we shouldn't focus on ramping up test scores, but on ramping up learning."

There was some applause.

"How do we do that?" the moderator said. "Fifteen seconds."

"Chess," Gorgoni said. "I waive the balance of my time."

"Could you elaborate? Ten seconds."

"Give every first grader a chess set. They'll be geniuses by third grade. I waive the balance of my time."

"Okay," the moderator said. "And the next question goes first to Congressman Gorgoni. The subject is transportation. Congressman, what can be done to improve the safety, efficiency, and overcrowding of our highways and skyways?"

"Trains," Gorgoni said. "I waive the balance of my time."

And there was a great deal of applause.

The momentum could be felt in the air in New Hampshire. Disaffected citizens who had never voted before were registering to vote, informing pollsters that they had been inspired to do so by Gorgoni, in flagrant disregard of the pundits who called his win in Iowa a fluke. Young people were flocking to him, attending his rallies on college campuses, cheering for him, opining to the press that his style was refreshingly honest. Young people were not put off by unpredictability; they were drawn to it, and no candidate in memory had ever been less predictable than Evan Gorgoni. They were talking to their parents, who may have been a little skeptical at first, but who warmed to Gorgoni after watching a series of debates in which he never appeared to hedge his answers or to dodge a question. Columnists were beginning to take him seriously. The state party regulars, who had been backing Poston, the home-state favorite, never could explain their candidate's stance towards the N.R.A., after the man twisted himself into a pretzel on the question of whether putting a stranglehold on debate was a good or a bad thing. Oakley, aiming to fill the vacuum created by an imploding front-runner, made a series of none-too-subtle digs at Poston—"I believe a candidate for President of the United States ought to earn his nomination and not expect to be coronated"—but always declined to attack the senator head-on, leading to speculation that he had really set his sights on the vice presidency, speculation that he denied in terms that managed to be emphatic and ambiguous at once: "Absolutely not, I'm running for the presidency, I have no interest in the vice presidency, none whatsoever, but you never say never in politics." Oakley's jabs at Gorgoni were similarly indirect: "A president has to be taken seriously and can't always speak his mind with reckless abandon," he said in the final debate, his head tilted ever-so-subtly in Gorgoni's direction. Gorgoni alone never attacked his opponents, and seemed oblivious to his standing in the race, declining to ever comment on any of the horse-race aspects of the election, even as the polls showed him climbing from third place in New Hampshire, before his victory in Iowa, to a distant second, afterwards, and then to within three points of Poston in the final weekend of the campaign. Never was obliviousness a more seemly characteristic in presidential politics. The people were looking for someone genuine, and only one candidate fit that bill.

Those who understood the nature of political momentum, therefore, were not shocked by the primary result that rocked the Democratic Party to its core. It was not the squeaker that most pollsters and most pundits were predicting. Evan Gorgoni ran away with the New Hampshire primary with 48 percent of the vote, with New Hampshire's own Senator Nate Poston barely edging out Senator Carl Oakley for runner-up, 27 percent to 25 percent. Of all the pollsters and pundits in the country, only Nate Silver of the *New York Times* could claim to have seen this result coming, by virtue of an algorithm that only he understood, yet even he had underrated Gorgoni, the day before the election, with his prediction of a blowout victory with 45 percent of the vote. Nate Silver appeared on *The Today Show* on the morning after the vote, and upon being congratulated for having scored once again as the most accurate political prognosticator in America, shook his head in dismay at being off by three points, vented some frustration at his miss, and vowed to go back to work on his algorithm. "If you can only get this thing completely right," Savannah Guthrie said with a wide smile, "there may be no need to hold elections at all!"

Nate Silver nodded his head in agreement and appeared a bit put off by her smile.

It was eight a.m., and they sat in the empty parking lot on the red-white-and-blue campaign bus that said "GORGONI FOR PRESIDENT" on each side, and below it, the words "NO RESERVATIONS." Only Monty and Gorgoni were aboard, per Monty's insistence that they get some down time together before the scheduled road trip to South Carolina. Monty was reading the *Manchester Union-Leader*, whose headlines blared, "GORGONI UPSETS POSTON," "OAKLEY SET TO ENDORSE GORGONI," "TIME TO UNITE PARTY," "POSTON CERTAIN TO DROP OUT," "BENNETON ROUTS IN REPUBLICAN PRIMARY." Gorgoni sat behind him, trying to solve a Rubik's Cube. Monty turned around and interrupted Gorgoni's concentration.

"I can't fucking believe we pulled off the nomination, and it's only January 14."

Gorgoni put the cube down.

"I know what you're saying. I'm starting to get concerned, too."

"How the fuck did we do it?" Monty's smile was so wide it exposed a gap where a molar used to reside.

"You got me."

Monty returned to his newspaper as eagerly as a boy returning to his new video game on Christmas morning. Gorgoni, with Zen-like concentration in spite of an apparent lack of progress, returned to his cube. It wasn't long before Monty turned around again.

"We got to hire someone to begin work on your acceptance speech."

"I'll write it myself."

"Well, someone to help you, to bounce ideas off."

"I don't need anyone."

"I'm the campaign manager."

"Congratulations. I still don't need anyone."

"We're in the big leagues now. You need a speechwriter."

"I got to the big leagues without one."

"Trust me, it was a fluke."

Gorgoni seemed to be doing better with the green sides than the other colors. Monty seemed intent on disrupting his concentration.

"Evan, with the nomination wrapped up, let's play it cool, stop knocking ourselves out hitting every bumfuck town in the country. It's time for the Rose Garden strategy."

Gorgoni didn't even bother looking up from the cube.

"You got to be president to use the Rose Garden strategy."

"Shit. Well, you need to relax a little now. What do you do to relax? Don't tell me wind-surfing."

Now Gorgoni looked up, and thought hard.

It was in Florence, South Carolina, that they found the dog pound. Gorgoni was disturbed by the size of the operation: room after room of dogs, slated to be put down if unclaimed, like canine prisoners on death row. Caroline held Gorgoni's hand as they moved wordlessly through the facility, observing her husband more intently than any potential new member of the family. Finally, Gorgoni stopped in front of a brown mutt with black spots that looked to be half cocker spaniel and half the product of a larger, darker breed, perhaps Labrador Retriever.

"That one," he said decisively.

At Gorgoni's insistence, Monty took a walk with him through Charleston's Magnolia Plantation. The magnolias weren't in bloom on this crisp morning in late January, but the daffodils and azaleas and hollies were. They walked along the blackwater swamp, past the cypress and tupelo gum trees, and Monty tripped over a boardwalk plank when Gorgoni asked him if he'd ever been in love. Monty said he'd been in love once, with the woman he dated just prior to meeting the woman he would marry and divorce; he described the experience as miserable. He said he didn't understand why people try so hard to fall in love when the state of being in love simply leaves one vulnerable and weak and pathetic. "I'm not particularly big on love," Monty said, and Gorgoni laughed. "When did you fall in love with Caroline? First time you laid eyes on her?"

"No. I'd say I wasn't sure until a couple of years after we were married. I just hadn't been sure but I liked her tremendously and I wanted to get married."

"Really? So then what happened when it turned into love?"

"Nothing. It was an unexceptional moment. She was in the kitchen, preparing borscht."

"You fell in love over borscht?"

"I *realized* I was in love over borscht. I looked at her, at the way she was handling the beets and the carrots and the onions, and I realized I couldn't imagine going through life not being in her presence. That her mere presence enveloped me in a kind of warmth. And it hit me that that's pretty much the essence of love. And when the revelation came that I was in love with my wife, that had to be one of the finest moments of my life."

"I'm happy for you," Monty said. "It's rare for borscht to play such a significant role in passion."

"You're never too old to find it again," Gorgoni said.

"Don't wish it on me," Monty said. "It's really an overrated experience."

"There may be nothing better than middle-aged love."

"Yeah, we call ourselves middle-aged. What are you, fifty-four? Are you going to live to a hundred eight?"

"I don't see why not, on my diet."

Gorgoni spotted an egret sunning himself on a log, and pointed it out to Monty with enthusiasm.

"Uh-huh," Monty said.

"I wouldn't have thought that egrets would be this far north in January," Gorgoni said. "I wonder if it's climate change."

"I couldn't tell you," Monty said. "Can we talk about the campaign already?"

"Not yet," Gorgoni said, and they continued walking in silence for a long while, past old slave cabins and the plantation house until they came to the long white bridge that spanned Cypress Lake. "I believe this is the oldest tourist attraction in America," Gorgoni said, taking in the view from the middle of the bridge."

"That's fascinating," Monty said. "Who do you want for vice president?"

"Oh, we're starting with that?"

"Might as well start thinking about it. You got to pick someone."

"I think what we've got here," Gorgoni said, "is a view that will give us perspective on that imperative."

"Whatever helps you, pal."

"You look at nature sometimes, and you shake your head a little bit at the things we humans find important."

"I get your point. But in most elections, it's mainly humans who vote."

"Let's not be cynical, Monty."

"So with all due respect to flora and fauna, I think we should narrow this down to someone who can appeal to humans."

"You got any ideas?"

"I got six."

"And you're determined to tell me who they are?"

"Yes."

"Go ahead."

"In no particular order."

"Right."

"Pete Dalton."

"I met him a couple of times, didn't get much of an impression, other than he's cautious."

"He's a businessman, very efficient guy, that's why he doesn't waste time making an impression. He's never held any office but governor, which is a positive because he doesn't have a voting record. We'd have to brush him up on foreign policy, but he's got that *gravitas* look. Minnesota isn't the optimal state, since it should be in our column anyway, but this way we won't have to waste any resources there."

"Next."

"Carl Oakley."

"Next."

"The unions love him, and women go for him. Missouri is a swing state; if we carry it, we almost can't lose. The man bowed out graciously and endorsed you copiously. He's already called me up three times, 'what can I do to help?' No question he wants the job; he's already campaigning for it."

"Next."

"So I guess we rule out Oakley, huh?"

"Next."

"Don Petroff."

"A general?"

"Again, no voting record. A great patriot, happens to be very progressive on social issues. He would overcome the objection that you're flaky or pacifistic on foreign policy."

"Sometimes I wonder if I *am* a pacifist."

"Well, add Petroff to the ticket, people give you a second look, and you get a shot at the military vote."

"Is he even a Democrat?"

"If he isn't, I'm sure we can fix that."

"It strikes me as far-fetched."

"Evelyn Hartwick."

"Superb senator; I've always been impressed by her."

"When a woman gets elected in a red state like Kansas and she's popular, that gets my attention."

"What are the negatives?"

"No foreign policy cred, and her husband's a jackass. A lobbyist for the online gaming industry. Which means that Sheldon Adelson may spend his last billion to keep the Hartwicks away from power. Plus she's on the stiff side, which plays well in Kansas but not on the coasts."

"Next?"

"Okay. My next pick is a guy who's overlooked in the category of national ticket potential. Drew Dunbar."

"Oh, I love the guy. Probably my favorite senator."

"He's a sweet man, very cuddly. Everyone likes him, everyone respects him, he's ready to be president. But he's got a voting record ten miles long, and the issue he's most associated with is gun control. Seniors love him, the unions like him, high ratings from the environmental lobby, but Illinois doesn't give us anything we don't already have. And some people will say he's not tough enough, just because he's cuddly."

"Number six?"

"Another governor."

"Shoot."

"Jack Hildeboop."

"Good thought. Jack's a fabulous fellow. Knows more about domestic policy than almost anyone in Washington."

"Yeah, he's a genuine wonk. Al Gore was even impressed. And he gives a good speech. He's disciplined."

"He understands climate science."

"Yeah, though that's not my favorite issue to talk about. But Colorado's the perfect swing state, and he's got a sixty-three percent approval rating after six years in office. And I'm more sure every day that the marijuana thing will work in our favor. But I can't get past the name. Is America ready to elect a Hildeboop?"

"Hey, there was a time when people asked if America was ready to elect a Dukakis."

"I believe that question was answered."

"Jack's separated from his wife, isn't he?"

"Yeah. That's a negative. But if they get back together, that's a positive. Women like that, shows that the guy hangs in there, works things out. Unless they think they got back together for political reasons, which would be catastrophic, so they'd need to do it right away. I can put in a call to the wife, she's a friend of Barbara Boxer."

"I have someone else in mind."

"Okay, who do you got?"

"I want someone I can trust."

"Absolutely."

"Someone I get along with and would enjoy seeing around the office."

"Okay."

"You know, we need to be a team. It's like a marriage."

"Right."

"You don't pick someone you don't even know. Ask John McCain."

"I hear you. And trust me, I've already narrowed the list to someone who can read."

Another egret—or maybe it was the same one?—flew low over the lake and landed on the bank.

"That's why I'm leaning very strongly in one direction."

"Which is?"

"My roommate."

"Jake?"

"He's smart, he's dedicated, he's got the back of the working people, he's on the Foreign Affairs Committee so he's up to speed on foreign policy, and he actually comprehends *Twitter,* so he may be able to help the campaign with that crap."

"A congressman?"

"Hey, *I'm* a congressman."

"Pardon me, I meant to say, *another* congressman?"

"It's the level of the federal government closest to the people."

"You can't have a ticket of two congressmen."

"There's no law."

"Only because they could never get it through the House. But it's an unwritten law."

"I'll tell you something about Jake, and I swear this is true, or else I'd never entrust him to be a heartbeat away from the presidency."

"What's that?"

"He's a class act. Every time I came home, I found that he always did the dishes. Never left them in the sink once. Not once. Trust me, that's the kind of guy you want for vice president."

The Gorgoni family introduced their new dog, whom Nicole named Wisdom for the way it barked whenever anyone talked politics, to their Bloomington home, around which it began to romp with impunity as soon as it walked through the front door. Both parties had been blessed with a truncated primary season this election cycle, and so Monty had suggested that Gorgoni and Caroline rest at home for a week, an offer they jumped at. Caroline cooked one of the Gorgoni family's mainstay meals for dinner—a curry dish with a fruit cobbler for dessert—and the family ate in front of the television because CNN was running a special comparing the two all-but-official candidates who would square off in the fall.

A photographic history of the Republican candidate filled the screen, showing a slender, good-looking athlete age into a venerable white-haired gentleman who emanated success, as Candy Crowley narrated: "Malcolm Ernest Benneton, sixty-six years old, scion of the family that founded the Rambling Oil Company in 1891. Graduate of Yale, 1971. Married in 1980, and moved with wife Connie to Roanoke, Virginia, the corporate headquarters of Rambling, where they raised three children while he served as CEO of Rambling Oil. Divorced in 1999, he remarried only a year later his current wife, Stephanie McMann-Benneton, a telecommunications lobbyist. After recovering from a mild heart attack in 2002, he funded his own campaign for

Congress, where he served two terms, followed by two stints as governor. His political assets: mountains of cash; strong backing from the business community, especially energy interests; presidential looks and gravitas; high approval among the Republican core family values voters; a united party eager to retake the White House. His weaknesses: he's light on foreign policy experience; there are lingering questions about his health; and he has a notoriously short temper. Running against him, Evan Nathan Gorgoni..."

And now Gorgoni's own photo album played out before them, its pages turning in a graphic that belied the two dimensions of the screen. Gorgoni was always touched and surprised to see how young he once looked.

"Born fifty-four years ago in Salem, Indiana, son of a car mechanic, grandson of a cobbler born in Naples, Italy. At the age of nine, young Evan would lose his father to heart disease. He put himself through Indiana University in six years instead of the usual four because of the time lost to driving a rig to fund his education. Taught high school mathematics in Terre Haute, then became a principal. Married Caroline Finley, an attorney. The couple moved to Bloomington, where she set up a law practice and they raised two daughters. Twice elected to the State House before moving on to the United States House of Representatives, where he was elected to eight terms before announcing his retirement last July. And then he was all but drafted to run for president. If elected, he would become the first president since William Howard Taft to sport a mustache. Assets: a nimble, grass-roots, web-based campaign, a down-home style, a reputation for personal integrity, and an intact, telegenic family. Weaknesses: a funding base dependent on twenty dollar donations, and a message that's a tough sell, short on promises and long on challenges, warnings, and explicit uncertainty about his ability to solve the nation's problems. Also, a lot of people think he's nuts."

Gorgoni shut off the set and beamed at his family.

"I thought that was fair," he said.

CHAPTER THREE

The Speech

*M*adam Chairwoman, delegates, Mayor Reed, fellow Democrats, fellow Americans, I accept your nomination for President of the United States.

I'll be honest with you now. Come to think of it, I'll always be honest with you. You may note the lack of a teleprompter. My campaign manager told me I'm a fool if I try to give a convention acceptance speech without one. He said it can't be done. I said, hey, Monty, you only get one chance to find out, maybe two if you're lucky. So while I'm not overly worried about giving a nomination acceptance speech without a teleprompter, I admit that it gives me some pause that my own campaign manager thinks I'm a fool. Thanks a lot, Monty.

What was I saying? Uh-oh. Shoot. Where was I? Wait a minute, it'll come to me. Hold on, hold on. Just give me a minute here. Oh, yeah, I'll be honest with you: I was looking forward to going back to teaching. My youngest daughter, Nicole, of whom I'm very proud and whom I love with a love that any man with a daughter understands—I've been blessed to own a double dose of this most tender of loves, the essence of which is, in your heart you don't want them to grow up—I'm sure the love for a son must be an equally precious thing but I suspect that the sons you want to grow up as soon as possible—my daughter Nicole said to me once, when I announced that I would be leaving Congress, she said, Dad, isn't teaching sort of a step down from being a congressman? Let me answer that here and now in front of the world. Should the nation take a daring leap into the unknown, honoring me by electing me as your president, teaching would be even a step up from that.

If I become your president, I can only hope it will make me a better teacher in the years that follow. There is no higher calling. There is no particular point in learning or achievement if it is not passed along. Q.E.D.

My fellow Americans, I stand before you tonight to declare my fondest hopes and deepest concerns, and it is your choice alone, and your choice collectively, to join me in those or not. I will not take it personally if I lose. Really, it will not change at all my high opinion of my fellow Americans. There might be, in my bones, actually, even a tinge of relief. But I have looked closely at the challenges we all face, at the problems that confront the nation and the world, and at the approaches that I would pursue in comparison to those that my opponent, Governor Benneton, would pursue, and I will tell you honestly, with no reservation whatsoever, that I will be voting for me. There are certainly some tough choices facing us, but for me, that's not one of them. My wife, Caroline, has given me permission to mention that she will be voting for me as well, and my daughter Mandy conveniently turns eighteen on November 1, and she wants a car, so it's looking good.

Folks, the time has long since come to declare an end to the age of ideology. It is, quite frankly, a nuisance. Let us stop thinking of ourselves as liberals or conservatives, Democrats or Republicans, hawks or doves, Keynesians or supply-siders, cat people or dog people, right-brained or left-brained, and let us remind ourselves that we are all human beings standing on a planet that is spinning on its axis and revolving around the sun. Spinning and revolving. Think of that. It will be hard for many in Washington to understand this, but it is possible to do two things at once.

We begin life by suckling at the breast, and so, in order to introduce to you my philosophy of governance, I begin with the breast. It is high time that women dispense with the mammogram as an annual ordeal. The mammogram as a screening tool may well have been conceived with the best of intentions, but they have gone awry. Currently the government of the United States pays for mammograms under Medicare and Medicaid, and it imposes burdens on the states to pay for them, and it imposes burdens on private insurance companies to pay for them, and therefore upon all Americans who pay for their health insurance. It is a policy based upon a fantasy, and it is a fantasy, however well-intended, that is predicated upon arrogance. Arrogance is never the path to problem-solving; humility is. Here is the arrogance that lies behind the mammogram: the conceit that science has arrived at a point at which, no matter how badly we may abuse our bodies by eating and drinking the wrong food, by smoking and using drugs, we can simply image the cells in our tissues and determine where a cancer is forming before it even forms, excise those cells early, nip them in the bud, and thereby save our lives so that we can go back to eating and drinking whatever we like and enjoying ourselves. A lovely thought, but in fact, a dangerous and delusional fantasy.

Let me give you the statistics. They do not lie. I've had to memorize these in order to make this speech without the crutch of a teleprompter. Here are the facts. 996 out of 1,000 fifty-year-old women will not die of breast cancer in the next ten years, without any screening. Again, that's 996 out of 1,000 fifty-year-olds, not succumbing to breast cancer by the time they're sixty, without screening. With annual screening, the same 996 out of 1,000 fifty-year-old women will not die of breast cancer. The number doesn't change. There is no benefit. None. That is an established scientific fact; by all means, look it up. It is a fact women deserve to know before exposing themselves to radiation, and a fact to which government has been oblivious because it is a distinct and persistent weakness of humankind that we often prove strangely blind to facts that contradict our cherished fantasies.

But there is enormous cost to this blindness that results in these millions of annual mammograms subsidized by your taxes. Many women will be given false diagnoses, told that they have cancer when they don't. They will be treated, with unnecessary surgery and unnecessary toxic drugs, and some of those women will be made ill or will even die from those treatments. Many will die of heart disease from hearts weakened by drugs taken or radiation received for cancers that they do not really have, or for cancers that would never have metastasized and might have just disappeared if only they had *never been discovered by unnecessary screening. Their deaths will of course be recorded as heart attack deaths, unrelated to cancer, but it will have all begun with a tragic screening of the healthy breast of a healthy woman. Many lives are unnecessarily ruined every year by the fraud known as the mammogram. And meanwhile, we all pay for this as we pay for other unnecessary tests and medical procedures while we complain about the strangely ever-rising cost of health insurance. As president, I promise to do my all to put an end to this fraud, the mammogram, and you can bet that the medical-industrial complex will be fighting me every step of the way. But I will give you a presidency rooted in science, not fantasy.*

What is the emotional basis for the mammogram? It is, quite simply, fear. Fear has driven us to impose upon ourselves, and in this case upon the women of the nation, a pointless burden. Free ourselves of the fear, and we free ourselves of the burden.

Everywhere we look in government, we can find the equivalent of mammograms: good intentions gone awry. Mammograms in the Defense Department and the Education Department and the Justice Department and the Department of Agriculture, outmoded thinking throughout the government. Ideas that may have been initially implemented in good faith but that do not work, and programs based on those failed ideas into which we sink vast sums of money. We need to review our budget through the prism of fact, not ideology. The nation can save a fortune that way, and begin to pay down our debt.

President Clinton famously said, 'it's the economy, stupid.' I say, it's the food, stupid. We need to eat healthier food, and stop being the sickest, fattest population ever to walk the face of the earth. Of course our health care costs continue to skyrocket on a diet so extraordinarily rich, so dangerously high in fat, so preposterously high in sugars, and so tragically low in nutrients. We can't go on eating the same lousy food and imagine that we will be saved by drugs and interventions. That again is an arrogant fantasy. The elegant solution is always the simplest one. Eat healthy food.

Here is an extraordinary proposition. Listen carefully because I don't believe you've ever heard a politician speak these words before. Health is more important than health insurance. I will do my best to lead our government towards policies that maximize health, health insurance be damned. I have witnessed all the endless, grimy, partisan battles over health insurance in Congress for the last sixteen years. There were times when I was so fed up with it all that tears would well in my eyes, but they were too bored to bother rolling down my cheeks. I'm done with it. Let's leave the mind-numbingly trivial subject of health insurance alone and fight the good fight for health. I will not judge my presidency a success if, at the end of it, more people are simply insured. Where is the victory in more sick, diabetic, obese people with health insurance? How absurdly low can our standards possibly sink that anyone would be excited by that outcome? That is not a metric that matters in the least when we speak of something as important as human health. Judge my performance by the metrics that matter: they go by names like obesity, heart disease, cancer, diabetes, and Alzheimer's. But the more we learn about these diseases, the more we learn that they are different expressions of the same disease, and that disease is the atrocious American diet. It's the food, stupid.

I met a farmer from New Zealand once, a robust, hearty man of sixty with a shock of unruly white hair who, on his own dime and out of boundless generosity of spirit, came to testify before Congress. He said that he had once been essentially on the dole as a farmer of apricots and cherries and plums. The government of New Zealand paid him very cushy subsidies. Then his government fell into a fiscal crisis, and cut back on farm subsidies. He was angry at first, even attended a peaceful demonstration of farmers in Auckland, but he learned to cope without the subsidies. And now his farm has expanded and it's more profitable than ever. He wanted those of us who serve in Congress to know that farmers would fight us initially if we cut their subsidies, but that ultimately it would be in their best interest, as well as in the best interest of the national Treasury. As president, I will take his advice.

Our government has been in the business for generations now of subsidizing precisely the farmers who grow our unhealthiest food with the highest demands for water and energy. That cost needs to stop now. We must wean farmers off the public dole.

Instead of insuring that wealthy farmers and non-farming landowners get paid enormous subsidies, let's insure that all Americans have access to healthy food. That is not the case in America today. Walk into so many of our inner cities. Fast food joints and liquor stores should not be the only choices for food and drink for any Americans. That is a disgrace beyond measure. There must be real food everywhere that people live in our great nation. If we are to subsidize any farmers at all, let us subsidize those who grow real food— organic grains, fruits, and vegetables—if doing so will bring down the prices of those health-promoting foods.

That spirited farmer from New Zealand made a compelling case against socialism in farming. I agree with him. There are times when we must simply let the free market function. But we must not make a fetish of capitalism, either. Show me the public bridge that pure capitalism ever built. We are a nation. We are a civilization. We will be remembered for what we accomplish together. To accomplish things together, we pool our resources. It's called taxation. There's nothing wrong with it. No civilization can function without taxation. If we accomplish noble things together, we should feel honored to be taxed. Let's stop bickering about taxes, and seek instead to accomplish together great things for which we'll be delighted to pay our fair share. Well, maybe not delighted. But we'll be okay with it. Really.

Let us acknowledge the imperfections of capitalism, for they are manifest. Most notably, its rewards are distributed in ways that are lopsided beyond reason. No matter how gifted an elementary school teacher you are, no matter how dedicated, no matter how many hours you put in or how many extraordinary extracurricular efforts you make, no matter the enormous difference you may make in countless young lives, you are unlikely to be highly compensated, and you will not earn in forty years of teaching what a gifted shortstop earns in a season of play. No matter how hard you work as a coal miner, even if you can survive forty years of coal mining without succumbing to black lung and the other dreadful diseases and the unthinkable accidents that plague that industry, you will not earn in forty years what a glib talk show host earns in a month of unremarkable chats with celebrities. No matter how expert an electrician you are, do not expect a lifetime of labor to tally up to what a hedge fund manager makes in a year, even a bad year in which he loses money for his investors. And if you work for a living at virtually any nine-to-five job, no matter how much you scrimp and save, no matter how wisely you invest, you will never amass a fraction of the fortunes that the sons and daughters of the shortstops and the talk show hosts and the hedge fund managers will inherit, not to mention the grandchildren and great grandchildren and great-great grandchildren of industrial tycoons. There is a class of people in this country who are so rich that it is a challenge for them merely to keep track of their money, and most of those fabulously wealthy people were born that way. Their fortunes were not achieved through merit, unless you find merit in being born lucky. Even if we subscribed to the dubious notion that our economy was orga- nized under a system of rewards based on merit, wealth would merely accu- mulate among the children and grandchildren of the meritorious. Capitalism breeds inequality like poverty breeds rats.

And so, even granting that capitalism may be the best system of economic organization ever conceived, the truth is that's a remarkably low bar, and we need to compensate for its many distinct failures. Most of all, we need to raise revenue through the fairest, least painful tax ever devised by the human mind, the estate tax. The other party calls it the death tax. Sounds cruel, doesn't it? But what could be less cruel than a tax that you don't have to pay until you're dead and can feel no pain? What can be a more fair way of leveling, even a tiny bit, the lopsided playing field of capitalism? I promise you under my administration a steep increase in the estate tax on fortunes over five mil- lion dollars, and that money will be used to build roads and bridges and to protect waterways and to help bring food into the inner cities and onto Native

American reservations, to invest in job skills among the unemployed, and to provide more care for our veterans and our elderly. All of us who benefit from these revenues will offer a deeply felt thank you to the deceased rich, and I'm sure they would say for their part, you're very welcome, and thank you in turn for allowing us to become so wildly rich with or without any real effort during our privileged lifetimes.

That is not class warfare. That is class symbiosis. That is a class love fest.

It's the working class that needs our help most. We need to increase the minimum wage by fifty percent in one fell swoop and then index it to inflation. Try to support a family on less than ten dollars an hour. That's indefensible. If we truly want to goose the economy, let's raise the standard of living for those at the bottom of the ladder, and ultimately it'll be good for those at the top. The benefits will trickle up.

My fellow Americans, I say to you with deep conviction in my soul, let us do away, totally, irreversibly, and permanently, with the leaf-blower. What a foul, execrable piece of machinery that is. To state what should be obvious to all, no human being should make his living wearing an internal combustion engine strapped onto his back. It simply makes no sense to burn fossil fuels for the purpose of blowing leaves from one yard to the next. Whoever invented that noisy, infernal piece of equipment should be promptly and unceremoniously blown back to wherever he came from.

But while we blow him away, let's have the decency to give a path to citizenship to twelve million or so of our friends and employees and neighbors who live in our country and are as American as you and I.

Also, we've got to stop putting so many damned stickers on pieces of fruit. Is that absolutely necessary? I can't stand stickers on fruit. I once bought a black plum—a small black plum—that had three stickers on it that said "organic." Boy, was I annoyed by that. I'll have Vice President Jake Busby look into the fruit sticker problem; this is but one example of how he will play a vital role in my administration. At farmers markets, by the way, the food doesn't have stickers on it, so that's another good reason to expand farmers markets and buy locally and save on the transportation costs related to food.

We need to get a handle on transportation. Let's stop raising fuel efficiency standards in the distant future, and start raising them in the here and now. No more patting ourselves on the back for kicking the can down the road. Let's take this year's most fuel-efficient vehicles, and make their standards the minimum standards for next year's cars.

We can debate whether texting represents progress for civilization, but texting while driving cannot be tolerated. My administration will come down hard on this deadly foolishness. Listen up, young people: if you like to text while driving, don't even consider voting for me. We will fund a national advertising campaign to educate those who need to be educated on this point, and to scare and shame those who persist in this stupidity.

Also, in a sane world, one-way plane tickets should cost less than round-trip. I will not compromise on that principle. And if we can't figure out how to make trains run fast, let's hire the French or the Japanese or the Chinese. They know how to do it.

Let's consult with the Dutch on how to protect our cities from rising seas. If anyone can help us there, it's the Dutch.

Let's see if the people from Singapore can share any ideas about how to keep our cities clean.

And let's talk to the British about how to reduce gun violence. They've had brilliant success on that score.

You can hear my admiration of the skill sets of different nationalities, but you will never hear me use the word "race," and I will never promulgate policies dependent upon the concept. There is no such thing as race. Let's put that foolishness behind us. There is no biological or scientific definition of the term; it is a fallacy. I have promised you an administration guided by science, and there is no scientific basis to the malicious notion that skin color should define a race any more than hair color or eye color or shoe size. There is, *however, of course, such a thing as racism. Racism depends upon, and springs from, a belief in race. Let's not encourage that scourge by accepting its premise that there exists such a thing as different races of human beings. There is the human race, and that's that.*

Affirmative action programs should therefore be reformed. They should be premised on economic hardship, not skin color or ethnicity. In a world in which we are all increasingly and gloriously mixed, it is only a matter of time before we give up on programs geared to myths. I see no reason to wait. I say to my Democratic friends, these programs will succeed more fully in their mission of leveling the playing field and encouraging diversity, and succeed without engendering resentment, if we focus on remedying economic hardship, and give up on creating unsustainable definitions of ethnicity. But let us not use the reform of affirmative action as an excuse to let such programs wither; let's reinvigorate this tool of democratizing our society by advancing these programs wherever we can. Let's double down on lifting people up.

Definitions matter, and where they are disputed, they poison our politics. The definition of human life underlies the debate over reproductive rights. Those who believe that human life begins at conception and who would deny women the right to choose to terminate a pregnancy must be forced to answer the question of whether they would make an exception in the case of rape. If the answer is no, voters can and will pronounce judgment on the morality of forcing a woman to carry to term the rapist's child. If the answer is yes, that the exception for rape must be made, we must ask how. Should the exception be made at the woman's accusation of rape, or must there be a conviction first? If you are going to impose new burdens on human freedom, the burden is yours to explain how they will work. I will oppose any new burdens on human rights, including reproductive rights.

I cannot imagine anything more foolhardy than forbidding people to love and marry whomever they choose. I've yet to meet a young person in America who would discriminate on the freedom to love. The future has spoken, and it is time for the present to catch up.

The freedom to love brings me to the subject with which my campaign has been most closely associated: population control. It has not come as a surprise to me that I have been roundly attacked on this score. I understand fully well that population control is not an issue traditionally addressed in presidential campaigns. I understand the sensitivities. I'm cognizant of all the reasons why few politicians have been willing to touch the subject in the past. I understand that I have more to lose politically than to gain by bringing the issue to the fore. I'm not as foolish, after all, as my campaign manager may think.

Let us consider the attacks made against my proposal that we adopt voluntary zero population growth goals immediately, and aim to permanently stabilize our population at levels about ten percent higher than they are today, in other words, at about 360 million. I have been attacked for being pessimistic about the world's future. Many have said that the economy's growth is predicated on population growth, and that without it, the economy would grind to a halt. I have been told that I am insensitive to the commands of religion to be fruitful and multiply. And I have been challenged on the supposed impossibility of putting my ideas into practice. Besides, some say, we will be unilaterally surrendering in a global population race that other nations will win. Others argue that I am assaulting American freedoms. Some say my ideas are just crazy.

These are the arguments made against me today with the population of the United States standing at about 325 million. I ask you, which of these arguments could not be made when the population reaches 500 million? Even with a half billion people, we would still be told that the population has to grow for the economy to grow, that religion requires it, that other nations have growing population, and that besides, you can't stop it. The same arguments would hold when our population hits three quarters of a billion and then a billion, and then two billion, if we don't all choke to death on our pollution first. Does anybody seriously believe that our population can grow endlessly? I think not. Just try parking in New York City today, standing on line for a ride at Disneyland, or catching a flight at O'Hare. No sane person would want to double the population competing for the same spaces. So then the only argument should be, at what point should we encourage zero population growth? A fair analysis of the crises facing us in climate, energy, water use, land use, waste disposal, food production, employment, and transportation suggests that that time has come.

If you believe it's possible for the population to grow without limits and to provide energy for that population by burning fossil fuels, I urge you to do what I once did: take a trip to Beijing, and ride an elevator up to the top of a skyscraper. Go to the window, and try to find the skyscraper across the street. You won't be able to. That's what happens to the air in a massively populated world of carbon-fueled economic growth. If you think that's China's problem alone, remember that particulate matter in the atmosphere is demonstrably apolitical. It pays no attention at all to political boundaries. Some of that particulate matter drifts over to California, and some makes its way to Greenland's glaciers, which it helps to darken and melt.

The good news is that population trends are stabilizing right now throughout the developed world, and so the challenge is to capitalize upon that trend and seek to export it to the developing world, precisely by helping it develop. Let us add more rationality to our planning, instead of more lanes to our freeways. We have to recognize that each additional million added to the world population now extracts a greater toll than did each additional million added a generation ago. That is because climate change is already upon us.

We have enough reserves of carbon-based fuels—oil, natural gas, coal— to warm ourselves for hundreds of years to come. But if we extract it and burn it, we warm the planet at the same time. That is our dilemma: we have it, but we dare not overuse it. It is as if we are being tested by an unseen force. Will we be wise, or shortsighted? We can drill, baby, drill, but then we will burn, baby, burn. I will establish the goal of America burning five percent less fossil fuels with every year that passes. There is no security in any other path. And let us commit that henceforth all the oil, gas, and coal on public lands will remain in the ground.

The world is a dangerous place. But it doesn't follow that it becomes less dangerous by placing our troops all around it. Let's bring most of them home, especially from places that we helped liberate three quarters of a century ago.

And for God's sake, how can we hope to protect people around the world if we can't protect the women in our own military from being raped by the men in our military? Are we to be as slow in remedying the crimes against women in our military ranks as was the Catholic Church in remedying its atrocities toward children? I will remove by executive order the military chain of command from the reporting, investigating, and prosecution of these crimes. Civilian justice shall investigate crimes in the military, just as a civilian Commander-in-Chief decides matters of war and peace.

The NSA needs to be reined in and to report to the president, not to engage in extracurricular activities outside the scope of legitimate security interests and outside the law. Surely it's not too much for me to hope that the NSA is listening right now when I say that it should have better things to do than to hack into the cell phones of world leaders.

It actually isn't as hard to fix our broken political system as it is to find the necessary political will to make it happen. Congressional districts should be drawn by non-partisan commissions, not gerrymandered by political hacks. And the Electoral College likewise needs improvement, but it's a complex matter that takes some forethought to deal with. Let's examine the conundrum.

We are governed, after all, by our Constitution, a remarkable, enduring, and revered document, but, let's be honest, not a perfect one. The Constitution establishes that the president and vice president be selected by electors of each state equal to the number of senators and representatives in each state. Since each state, no matter how sparsely populated, has two senators, this gives a slight advantage in per capita presidential voting power to residents of rural states. It is therefore not in the interest of rural states to switch to a popular vote for president, yet without the support of at least some rural states, no amendment to the Constitution can be passed, as three quarters of the states *must ratify constitutional amendments. And so we are left with a constitutionally unassailable Electoral College system and the reality that the candidate who wins the most votes may not be elected president. That happened most recently in the year 2000, and it almost happened again in 2004. It is a real and serious threat to the legitimacy of our democracy.*

But that's not the worst of it. The worst of it is that, through accidents of history, culture, and geography, some states have populations that are more inclined to support one party, while other states can be counted upon to support the other. We call them the red states and the blue states. Nobody expects Utah to give its electors to the candidate of the Democratic Party any time soon, and New York is unlikely to go Republican any time soon. Only about ten states comprise what have been called the swing states: states with populations that could go either way. And so every four years we have presidential elections that would look to a Martian visitor like elections for president of Ohio, Iowa, Colorado, Florida, Virginia, and North Carolina. Candidates spend virtually all their time and money in those swing states and a few others, while the rest of the country might as well sit out the election, as it's taken for granted. It's not a healthy state of affairs when it becomes all but pointless for a presidential candidate to bother campaigning in roughly eighty percent of the country.

And so here's the solution I offer. A constitutional amendment that does not replace the Electoral College with election by popular vote, but rather incorporates the popular vote into the Electoral College. I propose that the winner of the national popular vote receive an extra 21 Electoral College votes, and that winning the presidential elections shall henceforth require not 270 but 281 electoral votes. That will not make it absolutely impossible to win the presidency without winning the popular vote, but it would make it far, far more unlikely. Since every vote will in effect be counted twice—once in the state tally and once in the national tally—there will be good reason for candidates to campaign everywhere. Rural states would maintain their slight advantage in per capita presidential voting power, but now there would be a reason for candidates to campaign and spend money in the Dakotas,

Wyoming, and Montana, as well as in large states like California and Texas that are not usually competitive—since every vote would count towards the prize of 21 additional electoral votes. We would truly have national elections again. More Americans would participate, and that's unquestionably a positive outcome. The total number of electoral votes would be 561 instead of 540, an odd number instead of an even number, thereby precluding the unwelcome possibility of a tie that could send the election into the House of Representatives, a gerrymandered body whose current majority was elected by a minority of the American people.

While we're amending the Constitution, there is what I would call a mammogram, an accepted but dubious article of faith, enshrined in the Constitution for no sensible reason, and I humbly suggest we undo it. I speak of the storied right found within the Fifth Amendment that no person shall be compelled to be a witness against himself. Well, if you think about it, why the heck not? If someone you loved was murdered, and a man was charged with that crime but the evidence was somewhat ambiguous, would you not want the truth to come out? If he were guilty, surely you would want him convicted; and if he were innocent, surely you wouldn't want him to be punished for a crime he did not commit. You would only want the truth. To establish the truth, wouldn't you want to know where he was at the time of the murder? Why shouldn't he be compelled to answer that question? The goal of the criminal justice system should be truth, and this vestigial right does nothing but obstruct the path to it. I propose a constitutional amendment that will waive this right for all those indicted for crimes of violence, and for other choice felonies as well.

Now that I've set my sights on what I believe is an inessential and counterproductive right that our founding document has enshrined, let me take this opportunity to point to its opposite: an entirely wise and essential clause of the Constitution that has been ritually abused and ignored in recent years. I speak of the important injunction of the Fourteenth Amendment: "The validity of the public debt of the United States...shall not be questioned." Well, an awfully large contingent of Members of Congress has been repeatedly doing just that, every time we approach the limits of our artificially imposed debt ceiling. I will ask Congress to do away with the pointless debt ceiling, and failing that, I will invoke the Fourteenth Amendment to lift it unilaterally. The bizarre, unconstitutional argument made by the brotherhood of extortionists who periodically vote against raising the debt ceiling is that the president can always pick and choose what bills to pay without exceeding the ceiling: the interest on our debt can still be paid, they argue, thereby avoiding default and worldwide economic catastrophe. But in fact the president has no authority whatsoever under the Constitution to pick and choose what bills to pay. As president, I would be authorized to execute the law of the land, which means all spending authorized by Congress. Surely I would and should be impeached if I chose for political reasons not to execute some laws I personally disliked. Similarly, I would not as president have the power to arbitrarily choose how to navigate my way through an entirely unnecessary deficiency of funds imposed on me by a conspiracy of extortionists. Nor would I accept that power if offered. If the nation incurs a debt, we must pay it; no side may make the threat of default a negotiating tactic, or else the country will be rendered ungovernable. That is uncivil and un-American behavior, and it will be treated with the contempt it deserves.

On the subject of uncivil behavior, we need stiffer penalties for those insufferable sales operations that call people at home who are on the do-not-call list. One reason we have too many candidates for president every four years is that a lot of us will do anything to live someplace, any place, where we can escape those infernal calls. The rule of law must be extended to the right of people to live in peace in their homes.

Let's end the drug war. We've lost that pointless war, and the only winner was the private prison industry. Let's take the money saved by no longer prosecuting people for possession of marijuana, and the revenue taken in by taxing marijuana, and use it on educational anti-drug campaigns. Here's a good way to stop the drug problem: educate children about nutrition, and feed them healthy food in schools. If they grow up caring about their health, they won't want to mess it up with drugs. I have yet to meet a person on a diet of whole grains, fresh fruit, steamed vegetables, and heroin.

If we end the irrational war on the hemp plant, and stop ruining people's lives by making felonies out of victimless crimes, we can save the government a fortune, while improving the fortunes of our youth. No nation can hold its head high while so many of its youth waste away in prison, on the public dime.

Let us put the public dime in perspective. It is a shame that the accumulated public debt of the United States is so high, but it is hardly a crisis. We can easily afford to pay our bills. Our debt would be considerably lower had we not spent three trillion dollars to invade Iraq, a nation that did not attack us, but, oddly enough, most of those in Congress who rail passionately against our debt voted in favor of that misbegotten war. They voted for that three trillion dollar misadventure and they seek to compensate for it by trying to cut a few million from public television. And they seek to gin up a crisis in order to do so. Let us address the crises that actually exist: too many Americans are unemployed; too many are poor; too many are incarcerated; too many are poorly educated; too many are obese and sick; and, most worrisome of all, our climate is heating up and punishing us.

Our side stresses education; the other side stresses defense. The choice is ours to determine whether we invest more in the next generation of humans or the next generation of drones. Think it over.

I promise that I will not focus my energies on achieving goals that have more political resonance than actual human value. I will not knock myself out trying to balance the budget. I refuse as well to knock myself out trying to provide Americans with health insurance. Nor will I knock myself out trying to disarm other nations through the use of force.

But I am going to knock myself out trying to provide Americans with good education, good jobs, and good food. And I will knock myself out fighting for the health of the planet. In every battle, I will have reason and logic and science on my side, and I will fight with my all against the forces of hatred and intolerance and fear. At the end of the day, however, I cannot achieve *more than the American people wish me to achieve. This is not my fight so much as yours. If you choose decency, we will have decency, or at least a shot at it; if you choose greed, then it will be enough to do nothing and it will gladly swallow us whole.*

The other side has a simpler case to make. Trust in the forces of wealth. Let the corporatists have their way. Let the free market solve all our woes. Don't concern yourself with the choking planet. Disregard the warnings of scientists. Be satisfied with the dismal state of your health. Do nothing to lend a hand to your fellow citizens who are currently disenfranchised. Don't fret about having more incarcerated citizens than any nation on the planet. Let those who are sick and poor remain sick and poor and pull yourself ahead of the pack by starting a hedge fund.

It's an age-old battle. Greed versus decency. Ignorance versus reason. Intolerance versus inclusion. Fear versus love.

I have chosen my side. You have Election Day to choose yours.

My friends, forgive me if I do not close with a thundering voice and a grand promise. Let me close instead with a simple reflection. It is not given to us to know the significance of life. But we live as if it matters. We live as if it matters, and that makes every moment—not just accepting a presidential nomination, but walking in a park, holding a child's hand, brushing the hair of an aging parent, wading in an ocean—every moment is charged with meaning and purpose in a life genuinely lived. This fleeting moment now has resonance because the nation shares it, and shares it knowing that the future of the planet may be at stake. But simply walk in a park, hold a child's hand, brush the hair of a parent, wade in an ocean, and every moment can resound with the love of humanity that is our cause.

We humans are pop-ups on the earth. We should remember that every day, exult in the joy of it, wonder at the miracle of it, and observe the humility that comes with our status.

Thank you for listening, and rest assured that you do not need my help or anyone else's to invoke blessings upon this land.

CHAPTER FOUR

The General Election

H̶e was the first person Gorgoni saw when he stepped off the stage, after spending some five minutes waving to the crowd, his arms wrapped alternately around his wife, his daughters, and his vice presidential candidate and his spouse, his own smile far less wide and natural and engaging than the smile of the last Democratic president, Barack Obama, whose support for the party's new nominee had been notoriously tepid. Monty had loosened his red-white-and-blue tie and opened the top button of his white shirt, to the evident relief of his second chin. His thick features shone with flop sweat; his voice cracked with disbelief. He was, in a word, apoplectic.

"*Mammograms?* You used your convention speech to attack *mammograms?*"

"Read the latest study on them in the *New England Journal of Medicine*. They're worse than useless," Gorgoni said.

"Well, let's say you get all the votes of everyone who read that study. That gives you thirty-seven votes, which is about sixty-five million short of a majority, give or take."

"What I think Monty is saying," Caroline chimed in, "is that it's not really nomination speech territory."

"I can speak for myself," Monty said, irritated. "What I'm saying is, are you out of your gourd, pal?"

"I thought your speech was great, Dad," Nicole said.

"Yeah, what was your favorite part?" Monty asked. "Attacking mammograms or leaf blowers?"

"I hope we didn't lose the immigrant vote with the leaf blower thing," Mandy said.

"Then there was the stickers on fruits," Monty said, throwing up his arms. "There's a statement that will be remembered for generations! Schoolchildren will forever memorize Lincoln's 'A house divided against itself cannot stand,' alongside Gorgoni's, 'I can't stand stickers on fruit.'"

"We've taken them by surprise," Gorgoni said.

"Yeah," Monty said. "That's true. They didn't expect you to hand them the election tonight. I never heard Haroon curse before but he's scared the money is going to dry up. I'll bet every food manufacturer in the country is on speed-dial to contribute to Benneton, or one of his PACs."

"Don't we have a party to get to at the St. Regis?" Gorgoni said.

"I'm not going," Monty said. "I can't stand wakes. I told you to use a speechwriter!"

"Hell, we saved on that cost. I'm running a barebones campaign, remember?"

Monty's reaction to Gorgoni's speech was shared by most political commentators, who panned it as unfocused, meandering, and eccentric. Gorgoni achieved the dubious distinction of being the first major party candidate in modern history to see his approval numbers decline four points during his own convention. The New York Times, in an editorial, referred to Gorgoni as a "self-indulgent political maverick, more intent on airing his personal opinions, however kooky, than on constructing a coherent program of reform of public policy." *The Washington Post* called him "oblivious to political reality, in a way we find deeply disturbing in a candidate for the presidency." *The Wall Street Journal* called him an "anti-capitalist guru and environmental doomsayer masquerading as a political candidate." His broadside against mammograms was almost universally skewered as mindless political suicide. Republicans could not repress their glee, and claimed that Gorgoni had endangered the lives of women by challenging a valued screening test. A panoply of doctors was enlisted to make that case, while editorialists, columnists, and bloggers across the land accused Gorgoni of wanton recklessness. Most damaging of all, individual women who were convinced that mammograms had saved their lives expressed publicly their outrage over Gorgoni's speech.

And then, in the days and weeks that followed, a funny thing happened. Other doctors stepped forward to defend Gorgoni. Researchers verified the scientific data he had memorized and incorporated into his acceptance speech. Other women spoke up, at town halls, on television, on the radio, in blogs and on websites, about the psychological harm done to them by false positives on their mammograms, and about the physical harm of unwarranted medical intervention. Although public opinion on the efficacy of mammograms remained very much divided, Gorgoni's image as an unconventional politician willing to speak the truth as he saw it was gradually burnished.

Malcolm Benneton, by contrast, began to look increasingly stilted as he pursued a strategy of evading specifics on a host of issues in a transparent attempt to coast to victory. Benneton's handlers were so careful to make sure that he didn't bobble a lead that he was restricted to carefully scripted events, and a less-than-arduous schedule even of those. Benneton was taking plenty of time off, putting in a lot of half-days at private fund-raisers. The press was becoming increasingly antsy about the Republican candidate's unwillingness to make himself available to them, or to the voters.

After facing an initial, almost unprecedented deficit of over twenty points as the general election campaign was engaged, accompanied by a tidal wave of Democratic hand-wringing and even calls for him to step aside, Gorgoni had by mid-September climbed to within eight points of his opponent in many polls, as the base of the party began to return to the fold, while the oft-prophetic Nate Silver had him down by only six. The momentum suddenly belonged to the underdog.

Gorgoni did not concern himself with his momentary political standing, nor read the commentaries of the political pundits, but threw himself into the campaign with the same energy that he used to expend on reading policy papers. He enjoyed rising early every morning and, first thing, running for fifteen minutes with Wisdom, whose high energy and incessant, audible panting seemed to cheer the candidate to an extent that even he found curious. The run would build up for Gorgoni a hearty appetite for his morning bowl of oatmeal with fruit and cinnamon; the fruit was the only part of his ritual breakfast that would change daily, though his favorite was organic blueberries. A brisk shower would follow, and then he would dress himself more casually than most presidential candidates, wearing khaki pants and sport shirts, unless expressly instructed otherwise by his staff. He would then ask Caroline or Monty or Kalani where he would be speaking that day, and invariably was delighted to find out. He had come to love the country more than he knew, and whenever he got to see new places—Albuquerque or Scranton or Missoula—he wanted to scope out the town like a tourist, though he rarely was granted the time to do more, after a speech, than grab a bite, if necessary, before moving on to the next campaign stop. It was important to him not to be late to rallies and speaking engagements, and he rarely was. He and Caroline and Wisdom would return to a dog-friendly hotel late at night, where he would enjoy playing with the dog while reviewing the day's events with Caroline, who would offer her counsel. Hotels were a sacrifice for Caroline; she had trouble sleeping in them, since she rarely had the opportunity to open a window, and every day brought for her a new frustration on the campaign trail that kept her awake. Gorgoni and Wisdom, for their part, slept soundly, the candidate seemingly no more concerned than the mutt about his deficit in the polls. Then he would awake refreshed to face the new day with a vigor and enthusiasm that had begun to contrast nicely with the complacency of his opponent.

This day brought him to a town hall event in Columbus, Ohio, set up in a high school auditorium. He enjoyed town halls as a rule, but today's crowd seemed subdued, rarely breaking into applause.

"What are you going to do to rid our country of illegal aliens?" a portly, innocuous-looking fellow wanted to know.

"Boy, you know, the other side won't agree to amnesty, and you can't very well round up and kick out twelve million people, so we've got a regular Mexican standoff. I don't see an easy solution," Gorgoni said. "But one thing's for sure: fear and resentment won't lead us to a good outcome."

From the other side of the hall, a microphone was handed to a woman in overalls.

"Can you bring peace between Israel and the Palestinians?"

A handful of people in the hall let out a chuckle at the question.

"I wouldn't count on that," Gorgoni said. "Too many factions have no interest in peace."

"Do you think cities have the right to ban handguns?" a man stood up and asked, without waiting for a microphone.

"It doesn't matter what I think," Gorgoni said. "That one's up to the courts."

He was doing his best, but many of the questions seemed to him blunt, unsophisticated, overly broad, or lacking in nuance, and he felt that his obligation to answer each one quickly and move on to the next rendered the whole exercise a charade. Growing impatient, he struggled to maintain the smile and the relaxed persona that Caroline had told him would help him to win over the key swing voters whose support hinged on the most superficial of factors. He was a fount of energy, but if anything could bring him down, it was the disconnect between the voters' expectations and the realities that he understood too well.

⌒

He sat near the front of the campaign bus, which stood motionless in the high school parking lot. Caroline sat beside him, reading *The Columbus Dispatch*. She made a habit of reading the local papers wherever they travelled. Behind him, a couple of dozen reporters and campaign aides awaited the arrival of Monty, and then they would be off to Cleveland for an afternoon rally followed by a fundraising dinner. Guests at the fundraiser would be donating twenty dollars to the Gorgoni campaign—its self-imposed limit—and another twenty-five hundred to the

Democratic Party. Some in the press had accused the campaign of hypocrisy on this score. The campaign had defended itself with the contention that the Democratic Party could not unilaterally disarm, and in any case the Gorgoni campaign did not direct the operations of the party. Gorgoni had a tendency to wince whenever the subject came up.

Monty hoisted his hefty frame up the stairs of the bus. "Everybody out, let's go, let's go!" he said.

A collective groan emanated from the back of the bus until it was drowned out by the sounds of bodies rising, laptops being gathered up, and wisecracking from a frustrated press corps.

The pale, rotund bus driver stood up and turned to Monty with a quizzical expression. "Me too?"

"You too. Out! Back in fifteen."

"Should I go?" Caroline asked.

"You can stay," Monty said, biting his lip.

"I'll go," Caroline said. "I'm spending more than enough time on buses."

"That may be better," Monty said. "That way I can use the language that I feel in my heart."

She left her newspaper on her seat, kissed her husband on his forehead, wished him luck, and exited the bus.

The bus driver waited politely for her to leave, then stepped slowly down the two steps as if they were new to him, turned to Monty one more time and tapped his watch, then disembarked.

Monty sat in the aisle seat across from Gorgoni, ran his hands through his greasy hair, and stared at him with dismay.

"What's up?" Gorgoni said.

"Why do you think you got the nomination?"

Gorgoni shrugged.

"People *like* me?"

"You're fucking lucky, that's why! You were up against the gutless favorite nobody wanted and a lightweight pretty boy trust fund brat posing as a populist. You didn't win it; they lost it! Now you're the fucking nominee of the only political party in America worth a bucket of spit. Which means you've got a responsibility to lead. You're the goddamn titular head of the party. And you just did a town hall that will live in infamy. Your answer to every fucking question was, *'Gee, that's a tough one. I don't see what we can do about that.'* I feel like apologizing to the country that I'm partly responsible for you being the nominee! Every time you take questions, I can't sleep at night. Since the convention, our fundraising is down forty percent. Haroon is working his ass off but you're not giving him any help. People don't want to reach into their pockets to contribute to a guy who acts like he's in over his head! Do you seriously expect to be elected president by saying you can't fucking be bothered to do anything about anything?"

Gorgoni leaned back in his seat. He felt like a man at a crap table stunned, after an impossibly lucky run, that his luck had run out. Yet he had no quarrel with the indignation he saw in his friend's face. He had wanted advisors who would set him straight, and he knew he deserved this dressing down. Lately he had begun to wonder if he was not, in his own way, as guilty of coasting as his opponent. Benneton had been coasting by avoiding unscripted formats, while he coasted by embracing the tough questions that came his way and merely acknowledging the panoply of factors that rendered the issues of the day all but unsolvable.

"Huh? You think you can get elected with this shit?" Monty repeated.

"Probably not," Gorgoni said.

After the evening's fundraising dinner, Gorgoni talked Catherine into doing an end run on their security detail and darting out together to catch the second act of Stephen Sondheim's *Follies* at the Ohio Theatre in Cleveland's Playhouse Square. They had seen that musical on their first date at Indiana Rep, and both had a lasting sweet spot for its depiction of human decay. Caroline and Gorgoni shared wry smiles as the characters lashed out with wit at their crumbled dreams.

"Fabulous production," Caroline said, as they ambled out of the theatre, in between shaking hands with theatregoers in the lobby who stood in disbelief at encountering a presidential candidate and his wife.

"It really lifted my spirits," Gorgoni said. "I love the way nothing ever works out. Too bad we can't catch the first act tomorrow, but we'll be in Akron."

The campaign held an impromptu strategy session late that night in Monty's hotel suite at the Wyndham. Gorgoni and Caroline sat together on a black vinyl couch; Jake and Alvin sat in matching black vinyl armchairs; Melanie Ronceros, the campaign's new pollster, a thin, dark woman of forty whose red tennis sneakers nearly matched the wide red frames of her glasses, sat on a barstool, her feet tapping on its base; and Kalani leaned against a wall while Monty paced back and forth as he held court. After he administered a tongue-lashing over the presidential candidate's theatre excursion *sans* security, the discussion turned to Jake's role in framing the campaign message. Gorgoni watched Kalani's body visibly recoil at Monty's suggestion that Jake take the lead in shaping the attack against Benneton.

"So you want me to be the traditional hatchet man?" Jake said.

"Hell, they've got a candidate who never achieved a damn thing in his life except being born rich," Monty said. "He doesn't even work hard as a candidate—I've never seen such a fucking light schedule. He's trying to waltz into the White House. He practically takes every other day off. The man's taunting us."

"So what do you want me to say? We have Kalani to speak for the campaign in his own style; if he wants to do the attacking—"

"*It's better to have less thunder in the mouth and more lightning in the hand*," Kalani said.

Gorgoni looked up at him with curiosity.

"Hopi?"

"Apache," Kalani said.

"How's it going to play if the vice presidential candidate seems tougher than the nominee?" Caroline asked.

"I agree completely," Monty said.

"It was a question," Caroline said.

"Well, I'm glad you asked that question because I agree completely. We've got to stiffen the spine at the top of the ticket. And, Evan, it's not only about being tough; you need to *sell yourself*. Let America know that you're the only one who can save us."

Gorgoni reflected on that for a moment, and was aggrieved by the thought. "Well," he said, "at the age of twelve I discovered that Evan Gorgoni was an anagram for No Raving Ego. That's still important to me."

Some eyebrows were raised around the room. Monty rubbed his fist against his forehead. "Let me get this straight. Now we're guiding the campaign according to anagrams?"

"I have a natural affinity for them," Gorgoni said. "Monty Berg is Try Me Bong."

Melanie tried to steer the conversation back to practical realities. "Congressman, you're unfortunately underwater on leadership, on the 'Will he fight for people like me?' question. You're polling better on the issues and on experience and on likeability than on the qualities reflective of political passion."

"We're missing an opportunity here."

The voice was raspy, barely louder than a whisper, and supremely confident. Everyone turned to Alvin.

"I've advised five nominees in my time; I've never seen an opportunity like this. We can reshape the party in the image of a man who's now a blank slate with a good heart."

"But they're going to define Evan before he can define himself," Monty said.

"Which is why we've got to be crisp. Evan, define your message for me in one sentence."

Gorgoni smiled. "Come on, Alvin, the world's a little too complex to sum everything up in one sentence."

"The world may be complex, but campaigns are simple. That's what's so hard about campaigns—grasping how simple they are, honing in on their essence. What's your central, transformative belief? If you can't say it in one sentence, you're dead in the water."

The silence in the room seemed endless; all eyes were on Gorgoni, hoping for an answer that might help focus the energies of a campaign that they all knew was adrift. The motionless hush suggested that this could be the moment that would define their cause. Maybe this would be the turning point.

"There are too many people," Gorgoni said, at last.

"There are too many people?" repeated the raspy voice.

"There are too many people," Gorgoni said.

Melanie threw up her hands, and turned her gaze to Monty.

"*Oy vey*," Monty said.

⌐⁀

The first presidential debate took place at the Norton Center of the Arts at Centre College in Danville, Kentucky. Monty had coached Gorgoni to concentrate on economic issues throughout the debate, with a particular emphasis on the need to raise the minimum wage and create jobs by investing in infrastructure. The point was to position him as a mainstream Democrat, committed to a traditional Democratic agenda benefitting the working people of the country. All the campaign needed to do, Monty argued, was consolidate the base, and they'd begin to draw even in the polls, and once that happened, their momentum might be unstoppable.

By a toss of the coin, the first question from Anderson Cooper came to Gorgoni, and it was a softball. "Explain to the American people why you deserve to be their next president."

Gorgoni began by politely thanking the good people of Danville, Kentucky, and all involved in making this debate happen, "including my overly confident opponent, Governor Benneton." As the audience cackled a little bit, he drew a deep breath and went on. "We face a climate crisis. An energy crisis. A water crisis. And we're running out of landfills. Our schools are overcrowded. We have millions of people in prison. We have severe budgetary constraints, caused in part by spending on so-called 'entitlements' for an ever-expanding population. We have a transportation crisis—too many cars on the road, too many planes in the air, not enough airports."

Monty and Alvin were watching from Monty's hotel suite in Danville.

"He's doing it," Monty said. "He's making it the issue."

"Holy shit," Alvin said.

"I don't think he wants to be president," Monty said.

"...There's a single cause for all these problems," Gorgoni went on. "Too many people. Yet our tax laws subsidize having more children. We should make zero population growth our top national priority. Celebrate gay people and others who don't have offspring. The more we grow our population, the more daunting it becomes to solve our problems. We face a choice: more and more people leading more and more miserable lives, or less people leading richer, safer, healthier, more rewarding lives. I humbly ask for your vote because as far as I can tell I'm the only candidate willing to speak this truth."

"Governor Benneton?" Anderson Cooper said.

Governor Benneton, wearing an American flag pin on the lapel of his dark blue suit, at first appeared at a loss for words. He put his hands in the air and shook his head in amazement.

"I had a speech prepared in case I got asked precisely that question, Anderson, but I'm too astonished to speak. I'm plain dumbstruck. My opponent, if my ears don't deceive me, is attacking hardworking Americans for reproducing."

He turned to Gorgoni.

"I have three children," he said. "What are you going to do to me?"

"I intend to send you home to them," Gorgoni said.

Nothing else that followed in the debate generated anything near the buzz that was created by those first, charged moments. To Monty's relief, Gorgoni managed midway through the high-stakes political joust to squeeze in a reference to the nation's failing infrastructure while responding to a question about the deficit, but for the most part, the campaign manager's game plan had been effectively undone in the first two minutes. Analyzing the debate afterwards, Chris Matthews said to Lawrence O'Donnell, "I can't remember anyone ever before making population control an issue in a presidential campaign, can you?"

"It's a gutsy move because it threatens the one form of entertainment the middle class can still afford," Lawrence O'Donnell said.

"Well, he's saying you can still entertain yourself, just use protection," Chris Matthews said. "At least I think that's what he's saying."

"Not to put too fine a point on it, but if you're just entertaining yourself, you don't need protection," Lawrence O'Donnell said.

"Still, better safe than sorry, right?" Chris Matthews said.

Lawrence O'Donnell cocked his head to one side, and left the opinion unconfirmed.

The next morning, Monty retreated from Danville to the Gorgoni National Campaign Headquarters on Kirkwood Avenue in Bloomington. As was his wont, he avoided the reporters who hung around downstairs, and barricaded himself in his loft office, which a year ago had held upstairs seating for a pizza joint. Sometimes, Monty thought he could still detect a vague aroma of pizza and beer emanating from the walls.

Madeleine, a skinny, nineteen-year-old freckled intern wearing a tee shirt that could have been designed by someone in her grandparents' generation, with a peace sign in white standing out from a background of psychedelic colors, knocked on the door. Monty instructed her to enter, and she told him that a doctor was waiting to see him on some sort of very important matter. He told her to send him up.

A pudgy man of average height entered the room. He was in his fifties and had a crop of unkempt grey hair. His eyebrows were bushy and wild, a shade darker than his hair, and he wore black, horn-rimmed eyeglasses. All in all, he gave the impression of an accountant who might be slightly unhinged. He was holding a manila envelope.

"Mr. Berg?"

"Yes."

"Leonard Spacy, neurologist. Former neurologist. I used to practice in Jackson, Wyoming."

"How can I help you?"

"I got to confess, I'm a Republican, but I'm concerned for the future of my country."

"Wow, doc, you are just mired in contradiction."

"I've prepared a document for you to read."

He took the document out of the envelope, and handed it to Monty, who initially gave it a skeptical once-over, and then read it again slowly with growing interest.

"So this was around Christmas four years ago?"

"That's right," Spacy said. His voice was thin and cracked readily.

"And you're saying that this bearded gentleman named Mudge was really Benneton?"

"That's what I believe."

Monty perused the document one more time.

"Who have you presented this affidavit to?"

"I mailed it in to the *New York Times* and the *Washington Post* and never heard back. Even *Mother Jones* didn't respond. I didn't know who else to take it to in the press, and frankly it seemed more strategic to take it to you."

"Strategic?"

"You can leak it to whoever you want, when you want. I'm sure you have the connections that I don't. You can turn this into a time bomb."

"What makes you so sure that Mudge was Benneton?"

"I remember what he looked like, what he sounded like. He paid in cash. He never came back to my office, but he called to refill the prescription many times. I sent it in to a pharmacy in Laramie."

"And you subsequently lost your license because—?"

"Tax evasion. I've paid my debt to society. But I suspect that's why no one in the press will listen to me."

"Or it could be that your story doesn't hold water. That it's some kind of self-aggrandizing fairy tale."

"Be as skeptical as you want. I would expect no less. But the election could hang in the balance. And this is worse than Kennedy hiding his Addison's disease, if you ask me."

Spacy's voice squeaked as he uttered that last defiant sentence. He wished Monty a good day, then turned and walked out, looking humbled and rather miffed.

Inside the farmhouse displaying the Confederate flag, the man in the Pirates baseball cap was chairing another convocation. About fifty people had travelled a considerable distance to attend, and the mood was dark. Governor Benneton was, to everyone in the room, an object of ridicule, a spineless country club Establishment Republican who did not seem remotely aware of the imminent threats to the Union of a mounting national debt and a Democratic candidate who was, in their view, not just a Socialist but a radical, tree-hugging, gay-loving Socialist at that. Worse still, the Democrat, for whom some in the room had voted in attempt to saddle his party with a losing candidate, was, according to some polls, slowly gaining on the clueless Republican.

"I actually voted for that nutcase in our open primary," a woman shouted out to the chair, "because you told me to. Now I can hardly sleep, I'm so mad."

"You did the right thing. What state are you from?"

"Ohio."

"Well, it didn't make any difference by the time of the Ohio primary, anyway. Gorgoni had it clinched long before."

"I know, but this is between me and God."

"God knows and understands your motives. Gorgoni is dead meat, and God must be aware of that and pleased."

"So why is he only six points down?"

"Because Benneton is a pathetic excuse for a candidate. He's not a true conservative; he's just a big-oil buffoon."

"Why do we always have to choose the lesser of two evils?" shouted out a woman in the back of the room.

The man tilted his head back as if to showcase the mermaid over his Adam's apple, and, looking pained, said nothing for a long time. Finally, he made a fist and pumped it.

"The fire next time. The fire next time. But this time, even with that clown Benneton, if we elect a good Congress, we can reverse the drift to Socialism. Benneton is going to have to answer to us. Congress can control everything. We'll keep our Second

Amendment rights. We'll get the government out of health insurance and Medicare and Social Security. We've got a lot of good Congressmen who have never voted to raise the debt ceiling and they never will—and they definitely won't if the Devil strikes and gives us a Democrat in the White House. Gorgoni has to be stopped at all costs. Folks, there's only one reason a candidate would ever campaign on a platform of population control—only one reason, you can't deny that—and that's that he hates Americans, and he wants there to be less of us. He is one sick, demented puppy. The man's a menace to humanity."

He smiled, as the applause was terrific.

Gorgoni sat next to Monty on the campaign bus, reading the affidavit Monty had handed him. They had just done a breakfast fundraiser in Indianapolis, and were about to head to a noontime rally in Kokomo. Monty was of the opinion that the last *Indianapolis Star* poll, showing Gorgoni down by 10 in his home state of Indiana, was serving as a drag on the campaign nationally, and he was determined to reverse the trend in the state.

Gorgoni put the affidavit down on his lap. "You believe him?"

"It's coming from a crook. And it's a little bizarre."

"Yeah."

"But it would explain his light schedule."

The reporters began boarding the bus, and a tall, red-haired, freckled man in his early thirties, a rookie reporter for the *Bloomington Herald-Times*, decided to see if he could turn a bus-boarding into a press conference. He rushed ahead of the other reporters and dashed up to Gorgoni.

"Congressman, you're the first presidential candidate ever to make an issue of overpopulation. What do you say to people like me—I have six children—"

"Six?" Gorgoni said, his eyes widening.

"Four boys and twin girls. What do you say to people like me who may feel defensive on this score?"

"Nothing to feel defensive about," Gorgoni said. "I'm only raising an issue—"

"*A journalist with six children?*" Monty interrupted, astonishment in his voice.

"Yes," the man said.

"Man, you've been burying something besides the lead. Go sit down."

As Gorgoni shrugged helplessly, the redheaded man walked with a hangdog expression to his seat.

The fundraisers for the Democratic Party seemed to be piled one upon the other, and Gorgoni was growing tired of them. The campaign had earned its share of derision in the press for its policy of accepting donations in no greater amounts than twenty dollars, while holding multi-thousand-dollar-a-head fundraisers for the Democratic Party, which in turn helped to fund the campaign. Gorgoni had warned Monty that he would not hew to his talking points if Monty insisted on subjecting him to more of these shindigs with the well-heeled, and tonight, in San Francisco's Fairmont Hotel, he decided to keep his word.

"A meteor flies through space," Gorgoni said. "Take a snapshot of it at any given moment, and it'll be in one place, at rest in one location..."

Monty, Alvin, and Kalani sat at a table in the back of the room, dining on salmon and saffron rice. Alvin was the only one of the three who knew many of the two hundred high-rolling guests, and Monty wanted him there to make the introductions.

"Why's he talking about meteors?" Alvin asked.

"Maybe he's announcing a new space program?" Monty said.

"Could be a way to solve the population problem," Kalani speculated.

Gorgoni went on. "...But if the meteor's at rest, then how come, after the snapshot is taken, it keeps going? That tells me that the snapshot is a lie, that the meteor's never really at rest at all. We are that meteor. America is that meteor. And any snapshot of America, any image or report or poll or work of punditry that purports to sum America up has instead missed its essence, which is change. Let me leave you with one last thought. Maybe it won't always be the next candidate who brings that change. Maybe it will be the change that brings the candidate. Thank you very much."

The applause came a beat late, as if everyone in the room were busy reflecting on that last thought, but it was hearty enough, as Gorgoni waved and made his way to his seat beside Caroline. Mandy and Nicole greeted him and then headed immediately for the restroom. Just before reaching the door to the hall, they were approached by a man in a fedora.

"Good meal?" asked the man.

"The usual," said Nicole.

"Did you have the fish or the chicken?"

"Neither," said Nicole. "I don't eat dead animals."

"You're a vegetarian?"

"Yup."

"Anyone else at home a vegetarian?"

Mandy tugged at Nicole's arm, but not before her younger sister blurted out, "My whole family."

"Nicole!" Mandy said, as the man in the fedora smiled, then headed out the door.

Mandy was floored that Nicole acted unaware of the need for discretion regarding the family diet. Caroline had sat Mandy down years ago and explained how detrimental it could be to her father's political career if too much information about how they ate got out. But Nicole had been too young at that time to be included in that conversation, and Caroline had grown more relaxed about the subject herself over time. The family had shared with several of their friends their dietary preferences, with no repercussions. But the man in the fedora was surely not a friend. The two sisters chewed over the situation on the way to the bathroom.

"Don't you know not to talk about that?" Mandy said.

"Well, Mom once said it's nobody's business what we eat, but if somebody asks…"

"He only asked you if you had the fish or the chicken."

"Well, I didn't."

"Yeah, but you called them dead animals."

"They are."

"It sounds hostile."

"It's just a fact. The animals are dead. I didn't kill them. I didn't even eat them."

"You know what I mean."

"Did I just blow the whole campaign?"

"We have to tell Monty what happened."

"You didn't answer my question."

"I was being tactful."

"Who was that guy, anyway?"

"I hope he was just a guy, but I think he's a reporter."

"I assumed from his hat that he was some sort of private detective."

"So that's why you decided to tell him we're vegetarians?"

"Maybe it's not so bad. I didn't say vegans."

"Well, don't."

"What if somebody asks me if I eat cheese?"

"Say you don't remember."

"How can you not remember if you eat cheese?"

"When was the last time you had cheese?"

"Never."

"So how can you remember it?"

"Wow, you'd make a good politician."

"Better than you."

"Why do we have to live like we have some kind of deep, dark secret when all it is—I mean, Jesus, we eat rice and vegetables. Potatoes and lentils. Is that a crime?"

"Keep your voice down."

"I don't think Dad's going to be mad at me."

"Dad never gets mad, in case you haven't noticed. At least not since he passed out. Mom may freak."

"Too bad Mom never passes out."

"Nicole!"

"I mean just once, like Dad. It made him so cool. And now he could become president—"

"Well, his chances may have just slipped."

"Yeah. Would it help if I went back and had the chicken?"

"I don't think that would get him into the White House."

"Well, it's gross, anyway. I mean, I'd like to see him elected, but those chicken bones are disgusting."

"God, I was looking forward to having a White House wedding."

"With Frazier?"

"Give me a break. As First Daughter, my choices would be astonishing."

"Are you going to be serving chicken and fish?"

"I haven't broken out the menu yet."

"That's a shocker."

Nicole and Mandy found Monty polishing off Kalani's slice of chocolate cream pie, having already inhaled his own. They asked if he could step away from the table. He took one more bite and excused himself. The three walked into the hall.

"Monty, I'm sorry, I think I goofed," Nicole said.

"What did you do?" he asked.

"I told a guy I didn't have the chicken."

"Uh-huh."

"Or the fish."

"She told a reporter that the whole family is vegetarian," Mandy said.

"What reporter?"

"A guy in a hat," Nicole said.

"White guy, long face, fortyish? Did he look like a private dick?"

"I don't know what he's like as a person. But he kind of looked like a detective."

"Uh-huh."

"Is this some kind of big deal?"

"I think it should be okay. Thanks for telling me. I knew that your father was a vegetarian, which I wasn't looking forward to having him discuss publicly, but I don't think many people will vote on it."

"You should know: we're not just vegetarian—we're vegan," Mandy said.

"Shit," Monty said.

Monty found Gorgoni in a corner of the room, being buttonholed by a half-dozen Silicon Valley entrepreneurs imploring him to consider a new policy towards repatriation of profits. He made a vague excuse to take the candidate aside.

"What's up?" Gorgoni said. "What's so urgent?"

"I know you're a vegetarian," Monty said. "And I know you don't eat cheese. But are you a full-fledged vegan?"

"As a matter of fact. Nobody knows, Monty."

"Well, that's changed. Nicole apparently told Drudge."

Gorgoni paused, nodded, took a breath, ran thumb and forefinger across his mustache till they met in the middle. Then he smiled. "I don't think people are going to vote on what I'm eating, as long as I don't tell other people what to eat."

"I don't know what planet you're on, Evan, but do me a favor and take a snapshot of it sometime."

The journalist Eugene Robinson was analyzing the campaign on *Hardball with Chris Matthews*: "Governor Benneton has managed to keep his notorious temper in check, and so far no one has made an issue of his heart condition. Meanwhile, people are wondering whether Gorgoni has the intestinal fortitude to—"

"Gene, hold on, hold on," Chris Matthews interrupted, with a pained expression. "I've just learned that Matt Drudge is reporting, according to a credible source, one of the Gorgoni daughters, that the Gorgonis—the whole family, including the candidate—are vegetarians! And he's citing other sources who suspect that they're vegans! This is news to me. What do you make of that?"

"Well, I don't know. Clinton and Gore are vegans, they say, so maybe America is ready for—"

"Yeah, but those guys waited till they were out of office to go vegan. It's another thing to run for president and be asking for the votes of cattle ranchers and chicken farmers and pig farmers and dairy farmers and regular red-blooded meat-eaters, while you eat only sprouts or something. It has a negative connotation, doesn't it, to some people, the word 'vegan?'"

"It means nothing to me, but yeah, I suppose a lot of people aren't ready for a vegan president."

"The Republicans will run with this, I guarantee you," Chris Matthews said.

The upper echelons of the campaign had an emergency meeting in the candidate's suite at the Fairmont. Gorgoni and Caroline were joined by Jake, Kalani, Melanie, Monty, and Alvin.

"Okay, we got ourselves a shitstorm over the candidate's diet," Monty said. "The Speaker has already said that it shows that our guy doesn't share American values. See, these bastards—the less something matters, the more they want to talk about it."

Gorgoni shook his head with wonder.

"I'm running against a guy with heart disease and I've got to apologize for not eating meat?"

"When did it start—your vegetarianism?" Alvin asked.

"My old man died when I was nine. It wasn't long after, maybe a few months, that my mother turned us vegetarian. When I married Caroline, she was already stricter than I was and she taught me to give up dairy."

"Have you gone for medical check-ups regularly to make sure you're in top shape?" Alvin asked.

"I hadn't been to a doctor in a couple of decades except for when I passed out but Monty made me go, and I checked out fine."

"Why didn't you ever go to a doctor?"

"I never had a reason to. I've been eating very well, and I don't smoke and I hardly ever drink. I didn't want to ever leave my daughters behind the way my father left me behind. I take good care of myself."

"But you did collapse last summer."

"It was a hot day and it may have been some kind of heat malaise."

"What's heat malaise?"

"It's a combination of heat exhaustion with spiritual malaise."

"That's what the doctor told you?" Alvin asked.

"No, I coined that."

"I thought I did?" Caroline said.

"Oh, maybe it was Caroline," Gorgoni said.

"Instant polling shows forty-seven percent of Americans say that the idea of a vegan president makes them uncomfortable," Melanie said.

"As I recall, Romney had some choice words for those forty-seven percent," Gorgoni said.

"How do we handle the charge that you weren't upfront about it?" Kalani asked. "They're spinning it as a character issue."

"Schedule a press conference. Life is too short for this stupidity."

"*Life is the flash of a firefly in the night,*" Kalani said.

"Apache?" Gorgoni said.

"Blackfoot," Kalani said.

The next day's press conference was held at San Francisco's Commonwealth Club, and the national, state, and local Bay Area press filled the room to capacity. The chatter on cable overnight had been that the campaign was at a tipping point, that Gorgoni might be finished if he couldn't put out the fire that had been building around the issue of whether there was something fundamentally dishonest about secretly following a diet that excluded animal products. He knew he had to nip this problem in the bud, and so he let himself be peppered with questions from one reporter after another.

"Congressman Gorgoni, why haven't you been open with the American people about your dietary inclinations?"

"I never imagined it was relevant. If I get elected, I thought they'd be playing Hail to the Chief, not Hail to the Chef."

"It wasn't because you thought it would make you unelectable?"

"No."

"When did you become a vegetarian?"

"I was nine or ten. My father had died of cardiac arrest; my mother attributed his death to meat. He loved his steaks."

"Do you believe she did the right thing?"

"Feel free to ask her. She's ninety now, and in good health."

"Why haven't you shared this story before?"

"I have. With friends. Just not with the whole free world."

"Were you concerned at all about the political consequences of your veganism?"

"You know, when my great-grandmother chose to leave the reservation in South Dakota and move to Colorado, she took the risk of being hunted down by whites. But she simply couldn't accept being confined and she didn't care what anybody thought. So for me to care what anybody thinks of my diet—that strikes me as preposterous."

"Which brings us back to: why was it a secret?"

"There's a lot of personal stuff that's nobody's business that I don't talk about. Not just what I eat. Go ahead, ask me if I wear boxers or briefs."

"Okay. Boxers or briefs?"

"Can't answer. National security."

The room erupted in laughter, and the crisis appeared diffused.

"That was fucking masterful," Monty said.

"I was proud of you," Caroline said.

They were dining at Millennium, the celebrated vegan restaurant in San Francisco, in what felt to Gorgoni like a coming-out meal. They had invited members of the press corps to join them, though not at the same table, and indeed probably never in the history of the republic had so many members of the national press chosen to dine vegan.

"You were so good, I'm considering going vegan myself," Monty said.

"You're kidding me?" Gorgoni said.

"Yes," Monty said.

"You know what you did at that press conference?" Caroline said.

"What?" Gorgoni asked.

"You managed to shame them without their knowing it. It was charming."

"I never thought I was a charmer."

"You had me fooled, too," Caroline said.

The man drove down the highway through the wind and stubborn, near-blinding rain, headed for the farmhouse. He lifted his Pirates baseball cap to wipe the sweat from his brow. He was furious at the way the press had rolled over and allowed the socialist whose candidacy posed a menace to the nation he loved get away with not eating meat. Barely a follow-up question on such a fundamental violation of American values. For consolation, he had the bombastic voice blaring at him through the radio. He always kept the volume high.

"What exactly is Dimwit Gorgoni's agenda? He doesn't want us to procreate; he wants us to be gay. He doesn't want us to eat healthy food that humans as natural hunters are meant to eat. He doesn't want women to have mammograms. He believes there are too many Americans. He thinks we are not God's chosen creatures here on earth but just some kind of strange pop-ups. I swear he said that, he honestly did. I'm just sorry Gorgoni ever popped up but I guess that's his parents' fault. He wants to double the minimum wage, which would cost millions of jobs and probably cause a depression. He doesn't want to drill for any more oil or other reliable forms of energy; no, instead, he would try to fuel the greatest economy in the world on wind and hippie fairy dust. He wants to cut the defense budget, leaving us completely defenseless in a dangerous world. And did I mention, he wants us to be gay?"

⸺

Only a few dozen activists showed up at the farmhouse, attendance having been driven down by the storm. But that wasn't all bad, the man in the Pirates cap reasoned, since the weather had effectively provided the service of weeding out the stragglers from the faithful.

He had expected to chair the meeting, but was informed upon entering that he had been relieved of that responsibility by a thirty-two-year-old Iraq war vet who stood six-foot-five and wore military camouflage. He was given no reason for his upending, just something vague about a need for "new blood," and he was further irritated when the meeting was late to start. When it did start, the lack of focus was appalling. Too much time was wasted on local elections and debate over whether to appoint a committee to begin drafting a new Constitution, before the specter of the presidential election was even raised. And that's when the meeting finally came to life.

"This whack-job wants to stop us from reproducing!" an elegant man of seventy sporting a turquoise bolo tie shouted. "If we don't say no to tax-and-sterilization, then the generations to come will remember that—"

"If there *are* any generations to come!" pointed out a woman in her sixties with a high forehead and red hoop earrings.

The Pirates fan jumped in. "You're preaching to the converted here! What are we going to *do* about it?"

"What are *you* going to do about it?" the woman said.

"We're part of a national network that is mobilizing," the new chair said. "Every day we consider new —"

"Tell us one thing you're doing, other than more fundraising and I don't even know where the money all goes!" the Pirates fan said.

"We've got an operation in the works that's classified—I can't give you the details—"

"You mean the Augustine Barbecue?" asked the Pirates fan.

"How'd you know about—?"

"That's two-bit symbolic shit! I piss on the Augustine Barbecue!" As the former chair of the western Pennsylvania chapter of a national movement dedicated to Second Amendment rights and an end to the deficit, he undoubtedly had many of the same contacts as the new chair, so he was well-aware of internal national deliberations.

The tall man in camouflage looked frustrated with him.

"There are good people, on our side, making strategic decisions here who are more informed—"

"You sound like the assholes we're trying to fight!" the Pirates fan said. "Who are you working for, fucker?"

It was clear that he was wasting his time with these people. He stormed out, flipping the bird to the chair as he left the room. A few in the room applauded him. The man in camouflage tried to laugh it off.

"It's a free country," he said.

❧

Upon exiting the farmhouse, he reached into the interior pocket of his leather jacket and pulled out a thirty-two caliber

Crimson Trace Glock, pointed it directly upward, and fired without looking. The blast brought a half-dozen of the convening faithful rushing to the door, where they saw the Pirates fan hop into his Jeep, back up, and pull away with a screech onto the dirt road bordering the farm.

Inside the Jeep, the voice of Rush blared away: "Is Gorgoni a tool of radical Islam, or the Communists? That's what I admit I haven't yet figured out."

Gorgoni took Wisdom for a walk, accompanied by his usual retinue of Secret Service agents. It was a foggy morning, and the Space Needle was visible in the distance. His cell phone rang. It was Monty, so he picked up.

"There's a new Gallup poll out. You're down by nine."

"Gallup's been wrong before. Ask Romney."

"But there's an upside."

"What's that?"

"You're down by so much in Texas and the South that it's skewing the results. If we can distribute your votes optimally in the Midwest and Northeast, win narrowly in Ohio, Michigan, Wisconsin and Pennsylvania, you can lose the popular vote by two, maybe even three points and still win the election."

"That would be ironic, considering I spoke about how to prevent that scenario in my nomination speech."

"Well, the country can't say you didn't warn them. But there's no way you can squeak out an electoral vote victory if you're losing the popular vote this badly. You've got to get the momentum back and gain at least five or six."

"Right."

"And I'm hearing the same complaint from operatives all over the country. Haroon is like a broken record on this point."

"Which is?"

"You need to go on the attack. I've given you fifty lines of attack on Benneton and you haven't used one!"

"It's not why I'm running."

"The American people need to know that he's an oil company stooge. It's your moral responsibility to point that out. It's the only way to win. You have to frame the—"

"Monty, we got to dig a little deeper."

"I don't know what the fuck that means."

"It means we try to go to the core of who we are as a people and what we stand for, and how politics intersects with life."

"Look, Evan. Once you win, you can become a philosopher-king for all I care. Right now, we got an imperative. We need to drive Benneton's numbers down. That's really the only way we move your numbers up. After the spill in the Gulf, do we really want an oil man in the White House? Just a plain vanilla question to ask. No name-calling, just a legitimate question to ask."

"I understand the concept, Monty. We may have to agree to disagree on the timing."

"Well, there are six weeks to election day. We don't have that much time left. You don't have a minute to waste."

"I'll call you back later, Monty. Something important came up."

Wisdom had stopped to do his business. Gorgoni took a plastic bag out of his pocket and picked up the poop. With his other hand, he mussed the dog's coat of hair.

"Atta boy, Wisdom. Good dog. Yes, Wisdom, yes, you're a good dog!"

One of the Secret Service agents approached Gorgoni.

"Would you like me to take that for you, sir?" he asked.

"No, I got it, thank you," Gorgoni said.

Monty hung up the phone and angrily threw a dart at the dartboard he had suspended near the door of his loft office in Bloomington. The dart bounced off the wall just as the door opened and Kalani entered.

"I found a Mudge in Laramie," Kalani said. "Williston Mudge."

"What do we know about him?"

"Professor Emeritus in Economics at the University of Wyoming. Campaign finance chair for Benneton in Wyoming."

Monty looked up with interest.

"Seventy-two years old."

"On Medicare, then," Monty said.

"Which means that it would be a crime—Medicare fraud."

Monty smiled broadly.

"Oh, that would be a shame. Keep looking for—"

"I'm on it. If there's a photo out there, I'll get it."

His phone buzzed. Madeleine told him that Matt Drudge was on the line. Monty picked it up with gusto.

"What do you got now?" he said. "Too much fiber in his diet?"

Monty's smile faded as he listened.

Caroline insisted on spending a week at home with the girls, who were back in school. She sat with the girls in the den in the evening. Mandy reported that there had been a mock presidential election that day at Bloomington High North, which Gorgoni had won narrowly, but she was convinced it was a case of home advantage fueled by her own popularity.

"If he can't win Bloomington High by more than four points, that's bad," she said.

"We have to get used to the possibility that we may not be moving into the White House," Caroline said. "We can still be proud of your dad."

"You guys are underestimating Dad," Nicole said. "He knows what he's doing."

"So he's losing on purpose?" Mandy asked.

"He always taught me in long distance running to pace myself."

"I hope you're right," Caroline said, turning on the news, where they watched coverage of Benneton addressing a crowd of some twenty thousand in Akron, Ohio.

"Let's end the death tax and cut the capital gains tax and create ten million new jobs!" the Republican standard-bearer proclaimed. "My opponent believes that America's greatness is behind us. Well, get the government off our backs, unleash the genius of America's economic engine, and there's no limit to what we can achieve!"

The crowd cheered enthusiastically, and the reporter concluded by all but shouting into the mic that the Benneton campaign was growing more confident by the day, and had even quietly begun the hunt for an operative to lead the presidential transition team.

"C'mon, where's Dad?" Nicole said, to the television.

As if in response, the anchorwoman then introduced coverage of the Gorgoni campaign, noting that the candidate had drawn a respectable-sized crowd, estimated at five to ten thousand, to Pioneer Square in Seattle. Caroline and the girls leaned forward to hear what he was saying today.

"They say it's not possible to run for president without making false promises. Reminds me of the little boy in the classroom, drawing a picture. The teacher asked him what he was drawing a picture of. The boy said, 'God.' The teacher said, 'But we don't know what God looks like.' The boy said, 'You will in a minute.'"

A reporter in Pioneer Square concluded, "The candidate may not have roused the crowd to a frenzy, but many seem to have left the rally in a pensive, reflective mood."

"Well, that's good," Nicole said.

Caroline switched the channel to CNN, where Wolf Blitzer appeared, by standards unique to him, excited.

"We have breaking news. I repeat: breaking news. Sources close to Matt Drudge are telling us, this is unconfirmed, but as it's already been reported on *Politico* we're going ahead with it. Again, breaking news, and it undoubtedly means more trouble for the Democratic ticket ahead. Democratic campaign manager Monty Berg, who is running the Evan Gorgoni presidential campaign, Monty Berg has been accused by ex-wife Natalie Schinker of violent behavior in the last year of their marriage, allegedly throwing her down a staircase. Here to discuss the political repercussions of this breaking news: Mary Matalin and James Carville. Mary, what's your take on this breaking news?"

Mary Matalin tossed her hair back and then shook her head almost in pity.

"It's devastating, it's a death blow. With only six weeks to go before Election Day, Gorgoni is already down by nine in the polls, and now his indispensable guru, Monty Berg, turns out to be damaged goods and a potential major liability to the campaign. If he stays on and the controversy lingers, that'll hurt Gorgoni with women especially."

"James, what's your view?" Wolf Blitzer said.

"Who is this woman anyway?" James Carville said, his arms flying, his head slithering this way and that, his whole being contorted with irrepressible outrage. "Hell, this could be pure slander! I mean, are we going to let unsubstantiated hearsay drive out arguably the second best campaign manager the Democrats have ever had?"

"But will he damage the Democrats' chances if he stays?" Wolf Blitzer wanted to know.

"I don't know—see, I hate this kind of politics, and the Republicans excel at it."

"Now come on—" Mary Matalin said.

"No, no, no, see, see, this is exactly the kind of thing the Republicans do. They—"

"What about the way Justice Bork was slandered?" Mary Matalin asked.

"He wasn't slandered, and that was about a century ago," James Carville said.

"Not quite."

"Well, it was definitely in the last century, and ever since then, the Republicans have made it their reigning political strategy to create these irrelevant distractions, these diversions, from Monica Lewinsky to Barack Obama's preacher to some IRS agents in Cincinnati to Benghazi to Evan Gorgoni's vegetarianism, for Christ's sake—"

"He's actually a vegan," Mary Matalin said.

"You see, you see, they don't let up! Even things so irrelevant it's laughable! You see, Wolf, that's the difference between us and them. We're good, they're evil, and that's what it boils down to."

"Excuse me? You're good and we're evil?" Mary Matalin said.

"Basically, yeah, that's how I see it."

"I can't believe you said that."

"I never pointed that out before?"

"No."

"We never discussed that?"

"No."

"Okay, well, never mind."

Chinese food had been brought into the Gorgoni head-quarters, eight white containers with thin metal handles, and it seemed as if Monty had eaten considerably more than Caroline, Jake, Melanie, and Kalani combined. Monty's appetite always swelled with adversity. Besides, he had decided to test himself with a few weeks of vegetarianism, and he didn't find vegetarian food filling.

Jake had been in Louisville for a fundraiser the night before and was able to hop onto a private jet to the Monroe County airport to attend this meeting, cancelling a rally in Lexington, Kentucky, to do so. Kalani reached Gorgoni by Skype, his laptop set up on Monty's desk, and positioned so that Gorgoni could see all of them sitting and eating their vegetable lo mein, sautéed garlic and spinach, and Buddha's Feast.

"Hi, honey," Caroline said. "How's Seattle?"

"I had a nice dinner with Bill Gates."

"Is he endorsing you?" Monty asked.

"Yup. Not only that, but I'm pleased to report, he's going to give the campaign twenty bucks."

"Evan, it looks like we got ourselves another shitstorm. With me in the eye," Monty said.

"So I hear," Gorgoni said.

"The lesson's always the same," said Kalani. "Get out in front of the story. Get everything out today."

"I agree with Kalani," Gorgoni said.

"Monty, I'm sorry, I have to ask: where's the truth here?" Caroline said.

All eyes focused on Monty, who was using a plastic fork to stab a good-sized chunk of spinach and shovel it into his mouth. He let out an awkward laugh, mumbled something incoherent, shook his head, took another bite of spinach, and then put his plate down.

"I don't know where to focus," he said to the laptop, and then turned to the others.

"Don't worry about it," Gorgoni said. "Just fill us in."

"Are there any more egg rolls?" Monty said.

"No," Kalani said.

"Look. Here's the problem. The campaign's got a reputation for integrity, if nothing else," Monty said. "What are our numbers for integrity?" Monty asked Melanie.

"The congressman's at eighty-three percent."

"Right. I don't want to screw that up for you."

"Monty, just answer Caroline's question," Gorgoni said.

Monty looked straight at Gorgoni's image on the screen of the laptop. "I'm not big on love, as you know. Relationships were never my for-ti-ay. I was always attracted to depressives because I figured at least I couldn't screw up their lives; they were miserable already. So Natalie—she seemed right for me, at least at first.

But she started seeing a shrink and then it was one drug after another. Her paranoia got worse. When I started packing, she threw herself down the stairs, called the police, and accused me. After the divorce, I never saw her again though I got nostalgic once and drove to New Orleans to see my ex-house. Then she goes off the drugs, and sends me this letter—"

He took a wrinkled, folded, one-page, handwritten letter out of his pocket, unfolded it, and held it up to the laptop.

"Can you read it?"

"Move it a little lower," Gorgoni said.

He did so. "She sends me this…begging me for another chance and admitting that she pulled that staircase stunt."

"Well, that's beautiful," Kalani said. "We show the press the letter—"

"Get it out this afternoon and case closed," Jake said.

"Except now she's back on the drugs and nuts again."

"If the letter's a confession, you'll come out smelling fine," Kalani said.

"It's a confession, all right. But I think you've still got to go, Monty. I'm sorry," Gorgoni said.

"Uh-huh," Monty said.

"With Natalie unstable again, we can't have this campaign devolve into—"

"Right," Monty said.

"I don't think we'll lose Dems, but Independents get swayed by these distractions," Melanie said. "They say they blame the press but the bottom line is that a campaign can't get any traction with this kind of stuff in the headlines. And since we're still down by six to nine points in every poll, we need traction."

"Then let's release the letter to accompany the resignation, so Monty at least clears his name," Kalani said.

"Good," Gorgoni said. "Fair enough."

"No," Monty said. "We don't release the letter. I don't want to upset her. So I'll step down. Doesn't mean we can't talk."

Later that afternoon, Kalani faced a rabid press at campaign headquarters. As photojournalists snapped shots one after another, he delivered his prepared remarks.

"Monty Berg has tendered his resignation, effective immediately, and severed all ties to the Gorgoni campaign so as not to distract from the real issues before this country. He does so without wishing to comment on his ex-wife or her allegations. *Do not let yesterday use up too much of today.* Cherokee. Effective immediately, Alvin Vernard will take over operational control of the campaign."

"Is this an admission that there was indeed domestic violence—?"

"Absolutely not. *Do not judge your neighbor until you walk two moons in his moccasins.* Cheyenne."

And with that, Kalani made a quick exit to end the press conference.

Malcolm Benneton had the crowd from, "Let's build the damned pipeline!" The proposed transcontinental oil pipeline was popular here in Houston, and while the candidate's opening remarks talking about his experience in the private sector had elicited little enthusiasm, the pipeline meant jobs in construction and at the refineries—red meat for Texas. The candidate appeared emboldened by the crowd's roar of affirmation that seemed almost enough to will the pipeline into existence, and he used the opportunity to segue to his favorite subject: freedom.

"In a free country, that pipeline is a no-brainer. In a free country, the genius of private enterprise is unleashed to create jobs, to create energy, to create progress. I believe in freedom. Freedom to have as many children as you want. Freedom to allow them to learn both the theory of evolution *and* the theory of intelligent design. Freedom to live in a society where criminals are kept locked up, and where marriage is between one man and one woman!"

The social issues, Benneton knew, could always rouse the crowd.

At least fifteen thousand souls overflowed the Tom McCall Waterfront Park in Portland, Oregon, drawn either by curiosity or enthusiasm for the Gorgoni campaign. Gorgoni stood and marveled at one of the largest assemblages he had encountered, hoping that it was a sign of new and badly needed momentum. He wondered if it were possible that a critical mass was forming around the notion of the body politic facing its problems honestly. He felt humbled to play a role in such a movement. And then he remembered that the people before him were expecting him to speak.

"Look at the size of this crowd!" he said, at last.

The crowd roared with excitement.

"You can see my point," he said.

Caroline was in her bedroom, enjoying her last evening at home, before she would rejoin her husband on the campaign trail in Florida. She had kept her cell phone off all day and enforced a strict radio silence so as to lead something akin to a normal life for this brief respite in Bloomington. After speaking with Gorgoni in the morning, she had done her utmost to forget the campaign all day long—until now, while engaged in the rote task of packing, she caved in to the impulse to turn on the cable news.

"Yet another blow to the Gorgoni campaign has just surfaced," Candy Crowley was saying. "*The National Enquirer*—now that's not a source we always trust, but in this case, we've been able to verify at least part of the story—*The National Enquirer* is reporting that Dr. Gilberto Santos, a Brazilian-born Philadelphia dermatologist, was the first husband of Caroline Gorgoni, and that she married him at the age of twenty-one to enable him to stay legally in the country. If true, this raises moral and perhaps even legal questions. I spoke with Dr. Santos a few hours ago."

The fear that had occupied her for so many months was realized; her brief early marriage to Berto had been discovered; and suddenly her only concern was for her daughters. She sat down next to the open suitcase on the bed and practiced the deep breathing she had been taught in her twenties when she first studied Kundalini yoga. It had served her well over the years. Now she saw her first husband on the screen; she hadn't seen him in almost twenty years. She was struck by how hard to recognize he was, his face plump, his hair grey, and a grey beard disguising what were once the chiseled features of an ambitious, hard-living, gregarious, adventurous young man.

"Dr. Santos, you were married to Caroline Gorgoni for how long?" Candy Crowley asked the doctor, as he exited what appeared to be a medical center and headed for the parking lot.

"Two years. At the time, she was Caroline Finley."

"And was it a legitimate marriage?"

"Yes, it was. Now if you don't mind—"

And Dr. Santos jogged ahead of the reporter to his car.

Mandy, now seventeen, had come to join in her mother's eyes the adult world, while Nicole at thirteen remained a child in her eyes. And so breaking the news to them together was rendered more difficult still by their unequal degrees of maturity. But it seemed pointless to go through this pain twice. The two girls sat obediently on either side of her on the den couch, where she had convened them. Mandy sensed the seriousness of the moment at a glance.

"What's going on?"

"I've had this conversation with both of you over and over in my mind—I've thought a lot about how to say it over the years, and—"

"What is it?" Mandy said.

"Girls, marriage should be a big deal. It's the person you choose to spend the rest of your life with. But it can also be, or seem to be, in different circumstances, in circumstances hard for you to imagine, not such a big deal—a little deal, a piece of paper, you understand?"

"No," Nicole said.

"Well, some people get married to collect benefits—"

"What kind of benefits?" Nicole said.

"Pension, say, or social security. People get married for lots of reasons that aren't very romantic but seem to make sense at the time. When I was twenty-one and stupid, I had a Brazilian boyfriend named Gilberto, and I liked him very much. I didn't love him like I love your dad but I liked him—"

"And he was hot?" Nicole said.

"He was Brazilian," Caroline said.

"Did you sleep with him?" Nicole asked.

"Yes," Caroline said.

"So you sort of collected benefits?" Nicole said. "Is that what you're saying?"

"We dated for about a year, nothing very serious. And he was going to have to return home to Brazil after he graduated from Yale. He asked me to do him a favor and I did it. I technically sort of married him."

"What?" Mandy said.

"Oh, my God!" Nicole exclaimed.

"Dad is your second husband?" Mandy said.

"Your dad is the only real husband I've ever had. But my feelings for Gilberto were strong. I married him to help him but it was legitimate because we were a couple, sort of. He was a good man and I liked him as a boyfriend but I didn't love him. And I have nothing bad to say about him. He's gone on to remove countless melanomas."

"Does Dad know?" Mandy asked.

"I told your father on our first date. Of course he knows."

"Why are you telling us now?" Nicole said.

"Well, I've wanted for a long time to tell you both but I couldn't figure out how. Only now it turns out that the rest of the country just found out about it. So…"

"Shit," Mandy said.

"Exactly," Caroline said.

⌣‿⌐

Nothing made Gorgoni feel more like a solid, populist, working person's candidate than shaking hands at a train station, so he tried to work that activity into his schedule whenever and wherever possible. He was shaking hands at Union Station in Portland when a clean-shaven local news reporter who looked no more than twenty-five years old thrust his mic at him and asked, with a kind of bravado invading his high-pitched voice, "Congressman, any response to the story that you're Caroline's second husband?"

Gorgoni looked at him and smiled.

"And with whom do I have the pleasure of speaking?" he asked.

"Aaron Sudarski, KGW News."

"Aaron, I would have been honored to have been third," Gorgoni said.

⌒

The Pirates fan drove along, passing Baton Rouge in a thick fog and heading east on U.S. 10, headed for St. Augustine. Someone needed to upstage that barbecue, and it might as well be him. Rush's show wasn't on the radio, so he was reduced to listening to a lesser light, Bill O'Reilly, who didn't know how to crystallize his arguments as well as Rush. O'Reilly was too namby-pamby for the Pirates fan's taste, but still, he was making a good case now.

"Was Mrs. Gorgoni's first marriage a sham? It certainly seems that way. And when I say a sham, I mean potentially a crime punishable by up to five years in prison. It may be time for Mrs. Gorgoni, who is a lawyer herself, to lawyer up. I'll bet Congressman Gorgoni is sorely missing his personal Rasputin, Monty Berg, right about now."

⌒

A Skype conference was in progress between Gorgoni, who had just arrived in Tallahassee; Caroline, at home in Bloomington and about to leave for the airport; Kalani, in the campaign headquarters in Bloomington; and Monty, back home in Baton Rouge.

"Caroline, let's call a press conference at Democratic headquarters in Tallahassee at about three hours after your plane lands," Kalani said. "Give you a little time to catch your breath. Just tell your story, what you told me: how the marriage was real, how Dr. Santos had been your boyfriend for a year prior to the marriage; you gave it a try and it didn't work out. Don't embellish. Remember: *It does not require many words to speak the truth.*"

"Sioux?" Gorgoni asked.

"Nez Perce," Kalani said.

"Kalani's exactly right," Monty said. "You've got to respond right away. Don't let the story metastasize. They've already got that idiot on Fox spewing his bullshit that a special prosecutor should be appointed. For a marriage that ended twenty years ago! What a lunatic."

"*He was spawned in stagnant water,*" Kalani said.

"Navajo?" Gorgoni asked.

"James Carville," Kalani said.

Caroline was accompanied into the pet-friendly Aloft Hotel in Tallahassee by two Secret Service agents and Wisdom. A bellhop carried her bags into the room, which she entered with Wisdom, leaving the Secret Service agents in the hall. Gorgoni handed the bellhop a ten-spot, then, even before the bellhop could exit the room, greeted Caroline with a ferocious hug.

"I've missed you. It's lonely out here amongst the throngs."

"You don't know what I've been going through."

"I have some idea."

"We have to get ready for the news conference."

"We have an hour."

"I still remember the day Berto asked me, how I agonized. I must have weighed a hundred factors before I said yes. But a presidential campaign thirty years later wasn't one of them. God, I feel terrible. I feel like I just ran over a dog."

Wisdom looked up.

Gorgoni pointed at the dog. "Shhh," he said, stroking Caroline's hair.

Caroline looked calm and poised as she stepped up to the microphone without introduction at the news conference, her husband standing behind her, smiling, hands folded in front of him.

"Thank you all for being here," she said. "As I think you all know, I enjoy being out on the campaign trail on behalf of my husband, who I believe will make a wonderful president. I'm not so thrilled, frankly, to be in the spotlight myself, where I find myself today, because of my private marital history. But America has a right to know, and so I'll make a brief statement and then answer your questions.

"I had a boyfriend at Yale named Gilberto Santos, now Dr. Santos, a dermatologist. After dating off and on for a couple of years, he asked me to marry him, and though I was probably too young, I said yes, and we were married for two and a half years, though we separated in the last year of our marriage. We had a private marriage ceremony and it was not public knowledge among our friends that we were married. Yes, it was a legitimate marriage and yes, we cared deeply for each other, and no, I have never publicly discussed this marriage before because I did not until yesterday discuss it with my children. Perhaps I should have but I didn't know how. I'm a private person and I preferred to keep this episode in my life private. I can't imagine why it would be a factor in anyone's choice for the presidency but I'm happy to answer questions now."

"Were you marrying him in order to give him citizenship?" a woman reporter in the first row asked.

"We were twenty-one years old, and we had deep feelings for each other, and we would have been separated if Gilberto had to return to Brazil. So inevitably one factor among a hundred became that marriage was a way to stay together. Perhaps we wouldn't have married if not for that factor, or perhaps we would have. It's impossible to know."

"Have you stayed in touch?" another woman asked.

"Intermittently."

"Why did you divorce?" a male reporter asked.

"Wow," Caroline said. "Did you actually ask me that? Is nothing private anymore? Next question."

"Congressman, do you know Dr. Santos?"

Gorgoni stepped forward and put his arm around Caroline. "Yes, I met Dr. Santos about fifteen years ago."

"What did you think of him?"

"I thought he was a fine fellow. I'm pleased to have him for an ex-husband-in-law."

"Was the campaign trying to keep the record of this marriage a secret?"

"I believe my wife just explained that she's a private person and this marriage was not something she ever chose to talk about.

I am trying to conduct a campaign for president of the United States, and we have had a non-stop series of distractions concerning things like the food I choose to eat, or allegations made by my former campaign manager's ex-wife, or my wife's romantic history in her early twenties. I would challenge the press to try instead to go off on a whole new tangent by actually drawing out the candidates on the concerns of the American people. I think Caroline has answered whatever marginally relevant questions might exist about this current silly distraction, and now we will move on with the campaign. Thank you very much."

Gorgoni escorted Caroline from the podium, but not before someone in room shouted out, "Is Dr. Santos also a vegan?"

While dissenting views were expressed on Fox News, the consensus in the media was that the Gorgonis' press conference had effectively nipped a new crisis in the bud and precluded the subject of Caroline's first marriage from taking wing. Caroline began to relax that evening in the hotel, and at night made love to her husband with a passion that had been missing since the start of the presidential campaign.

"What just happened?" Gorgoni said, rolling over onto his back after climaxing.

"If you don't know, I'm not sure you're qualified for the presidency," Caroline said.

"Well, it's been awhile," Gorgoni said. "You didn't seem interested for a long time."

"I didn't want to dissipate your energy," Caroline said.

"A misperception," Gorgoni said. "It contributes to male energy. Wait till you see me campaign tomorrow."

"Well, I didn't want you to win too easily."

They were awakened by the hotel clock alarm at a quarter to six, Gloria Estefan crooning *Mi Buen Amor.*

"Oh, God, how many events today?" Caroline said, rolling over onto her back.

Gorgoni struggled with the alarm clock, the voice of Gloria Estefan oblivious to his efforts.

"Orlando, Daytona, and that parade in St. Augustine. How do you shut this thing off?"

Wisdom began to howl along with the music. Gorgoni decided to let the Latin love song play on, and listened to Wisdom in amazement. Caroline bolted up to watch Wisdom as he howled to the music.

"Could Wisdom be the thing that sings?" Gorgoni asked.

Monty now watched the Sunday morning news shows from the comfort of his home in Baton Rouge. Alvin had officially taken over the reins of the campaign, but he consulted with Monty regularly, and always after the Sunday morning shows. In his own mind, at least, Monty believed he was still running the campaign, however indirectly. His "firing" had simply meant a lower level of stress and time commitment, a change of location, and of course no salary. He grimaced as George Stephanopoulos began a discussion of the presidential race by focusing on the polls.

"Let me begin by asking the Roundtable," George Stephanopoulos said, "with Benneton leading Gorgoni by eight to ten points in the polls, is it effectively over?"

"Congressman Gorgoni, bless his heart, has been a paragon of consistency," George Will said. "Consistently negative and consistently strange, and I simply don't believe that the American people will ever rally to the great cause of despair."

"Well, I agree with George," Cokie Roberts said. "It was a cute act at first to be the contrary candidate, to all but advertise his inability to solve a host of problems, to choose another scarcely known congressman, Jake Busby, for Vice President, but at the end of the day, population limits and climate change—these aren't issues that people vote on."

"Arianna?" George Stephanopoulos said.

"Don't make the mistake of counting Evan Gorgoni out," Arianna Huffington said. "He's still raking in Googles of money over the web, twenty bucks at a time, letting Benneton saturate the airwaves with attack ads while Gorgoni runs a subversive campaign over social media, on networking sites and *YouTube*—"

"*YouTube* isn't the weapon you need when you're trailing by eight with less than a month to go," Bill Kristol said. "Gorgoni's campaign has been plagued by scandal, and if he doesn't energize his base and convert a ton of independents in the final debate in Tampa, he's finished, if he isn't finished already."

When Alvin called, Monty reassured him that, in his experience, Bill Kristol was unfailingly wrong. "This is the same guy who said the Iraq war would be a cakewalk and the Sunnis and Shia would get along fine. The man holds the world record for never predicting anything right. Joe

DiMaggio's hitting streak will be broken before Bill Kristol's missing streak. So I'm glad he thinks we're finished. It gives me hope."

⟨⟩

The Columbus Day Parade down St. George Street in St. Augustine was a motley affair, seemingly disorganized and random, with a couple of marching bands playing patriotic songs; some people dressed as explorers; some people dressed as Native Americans; a small, peaceful protest being conducted by actual Native Americans; young people handing out flyers, hawking local businesses; a contingent of old veterans dressed in uniform; and the whole atmosphere supercharged by the presence of a presidential candidate and his wife just a few weeks before election day. It was a sunny, warm fall afternoon, and Gorgoni and Caroline ambled along in the middle of the parade, waving, shaking hands, and stopping to chat with anyone who rushed into the parade to greet them. Now coming into their view were the twin stone columns, the Old City Gates, at the north end of St. George Street, the endpoint of the parade.

"Are you as hungry as I am?" Gorgoni asked.

"I could go for a burrito. Think we could get a burrito around here?" Caroline said.

"I'm pretty sure. The Spanish settled this place."

"What the hell's going on?"

There was alarm in Caroline's tone, and Gorgoni followed her gaze to the City Gates. There, a van had stopped, blocking the exit of the parade participants, and four men in ski masks jumped from the van. The men unfurled a banner across the span between the stone columns and tied it with rope to those columns. The banner read:

SAVE THE UNBORN
SAVE THE LIVING
DEFEAT GORGONI

Banner in place, the four operatives then suspended a life-sized effigy—a mustachioed straw man clad in red, a carrot in his mouth—of Gorgoni beneath it, and set it aflame. Then they jumped back into their van and sped off.

Not a minute later, a white-haired man carrying a fire extinguisher ran out of a St. George Street café towards the burning effigy, and snuffed out the flame in an instant.

Their Secret Service men pulled Caroline and Gorgoni back several yards, away from the commotion, though it was Gorgoni's instinct to move towards it. Police sirens could be heard and two policemen were already tearing down the banner at the City Gates. Several of the participants in the parade fled to the sides of the street as if for safety, although there was no discernable threat once the van had left the scene.

To all appearances, it was a highly planned stunt that had fizzled immediately. But the excitement was not entirely over, as a man whose neck and arms were covered in tattoos, and who sported a Pirates baseball cap, ran into the center of the street, not five yards from Gorgoni, and unleashed at him a rage that seemed to the candidate almost beyond imagining.

"WHY DO YOU HATE AMERICA? WHY DO YOU HATE AMERICA?" he shouted, his face red with fury, his index finger pointing at Gorgoni, his thumb vertical, the image of a gun.

Two Secret Service men, each about six-foot-three, were on top of the Pirates fan before he could react, each grabbing one of the man's arms.

Gorgoni walked a step towards him.

"That's okay, he's not going to hurt me. You're not planning to hurt anyone, are you?" he asked the man in the Pirates cap.

"This is America! I have free speech!" the man shouted.

"That's right. Let him go," Gorgoni instructed the Secret Service men, who loosened their grip on the man, but did not release him entirely. Two other Secret Service men held the crowd back, for this live confrontation had quickly drawn attention away from the sight of the burnt straw man, drowned in foam. "Now can you lower the volume, sir? Can we talk this out?"

"Tell us why you hate America!" the Pirates fan said.

"Where in the world did you get that idea?" Gorgoni asked.

"You want to raise taxes—"

"On millionaires. Are you a millionaire?"

"I will be. One day."

"Good for you. If you don't mind my asking, how are you going to do it?"

"Gonna start a business."

"Excellent. What kind of business."

The Pirates fan hesitated, as if searching for an objection to this line of questioning; but unable to locate one, he answered in a low tone.

"Fishing tackle."

"I'm lowering taxes on small businesses, which will help you succeed—then, once you're making a cool mil, would you mind giving back a little to help pay down our debt? Is that un-American?"

"No, but—"

"There you go. My point exactly. Give me a hug."

Gorgoni extended his arms for a hug, to the evident alarm of his Secret Service retinue.

The Pirates fan revived his anger. "Go to hell, I'm not gonna—"

"Okay, tell you what," Gorgoni said. "When I'm elected, you come to the Rose Garden, and we can discuss whatever misgivings you may have with my philosophy of governance. I look forward to a brisk exchange of ideas. That's what America's about, isn't it? How's that sound?"

Gorgoni extended his hand. The Pirates fan looked around and saw faces that did not look as angry as his own, faces that seemed to appreciate the candidate's tone, faces celebrating normalcy and civility, faces silently urging him to shake the candidate's hand. Without knowing why, he found himself doing just that.

"Good man," Gorgoni said. "I appreciate your civic activism. Give us your contact information and we'll keep in touch. I wish you all the best with the fishing tackle business."

As Secret Service men took the Pirates fan aside for questioning, Gorgoni and Caroline moved along with the parade, as a high school marching band behind them picked up its rendition of *The Stars and Stripes Forever.*

Media coverage of the St. Augustine protest, which Rachel Maddow dubbed "Gate Gate," was fairly light, overshadowed by another event in the campaign that happened only some ninety minutes later, at Schenley Park in Pittsburgh. There, as Benneton waved to a crowd of six thousand chanting his name and holding mostly friendly placards, he was seen to close his eyes. His waving ceased, his eyes remained closed for several seconds, and then he started to fall backwards. A Secret Service agent steadied him, and moments later he was restored to consciousness. He returned to the podium, smiled, and regained his composure.

"Sorry, folks, that was nothing. Don't worry. Just campaigning long and hard," he said.

Gorgoni watched the coverage of the apparent fainting spell in his hotel suite, having first learned of it in an excited phone call from Alvin. His immediate, instinctual reaction was that neither he nor his campaign should comment upon it or play it up as an issue of concern. To do so would be tacky, and would risk having the thing blow up in their faces. He would leave it alone, as a matter of decency. And yet, seeing now on the screen the image of Benneton falling backwards, he felt that it looked odd and almost inexplicable. Caroline, resting her head on his chest, looked up at him and smiled.

Chuck Todd reported that Benneton's campaign explained that the governor was suffering from "exhaustion after a grueling campaign schedule."

"Grueling my ass," Caroline said.

The next morning began with an unscheduled, emergency Skype conference called by Alvin: Gorgoni and Caroline in their hotel suite; Monty back home in Baton Rouge; Alvin and Kalani in the campaign headquarters in Bloomington; and Jake in his hotel suite in Denver.

"Okay, what do you got?" Monty said. He was unshaven, puffy-eyed, and had wrapped himself in a frayed blue bathrobe.

"Kalani unearthed a photo," Alvin said.

"*Richmond Times-Dispatch*, December 18, 2006, Benneton's first year as governor," Kalani said. One day before the date cited in the affidavit. He's sporting a white beard."

"Beautiful," said Monty.

"He's ducking into his car, could be on the way to the airport," Kalani said. Kalani held the photo up to his computer monitor's camera, and the grainy image was visible to the other partipants in the call. "The governor's office didn't announce any trip, but he wasn't seen in public for two weeks."

"So, let's see," Monty said. "We got the affidavit from Spacy about a bearded guy named Mudge who he believes was Benneton, coming to his office to treat narcolepsy. We got a photo, taken the day before, of Benneton in a beard that he's never worn in his public life. We got a senior citizen named Mudge in Jackson, Wyoming, who's helping finance his campaign, and we've got the candidate actually falling asleep in front of a crowd, in the middle of the lightest campaign schedule since Stalin's reelection of 1936. What are we waiting for?"

"Do we want a president asleep at the switch?" Alvin asked.

"Literally," Caroline said.

"The whole thing makes me queasy," Gorgoni said.

"Respectfully, Evan, respectfully, let me say this in as nuanced a way as I can: *are you fucking kidding me?*" Monty said. "It's your patriotic duty to save us all from a man who could be fast asleep if the country was attacked at high noon! I'm sorry, but narcolepsy disqualifies a person from being President of the United States."

"So does lying about it," Kalani said.

"And committing Medicare fraud," Jake said.

"Thank you," Monty said.

"Evan, we've got to attack on this," Jake said. "You know how much I respect your self-restraint, but in this case, to not tell the American people what we know would mean effectively participating in a cover-up. It would be unforgivable." He spoke these words with the conviction of a friend and confidant, and it was apparent to all that they had an immediate effect on Gorgoni.

But Gorgoni said nothing, only rubbed his fingers along his mustache, deep in thought. There was an awkward Skype silence.

"Better yet," Monty said, filling the void, "we just leak it to the press."

"Much better," Caroline said.

"No," Gorgoni said. "That's the coward's way out. I'll do it myself."

Alvin arranged for the Gorgoni family to stay at a golf resort just outside of Tampa in preparation for the final debate, the event that virtually all political prognosticators referred to as the last hope of the Gorgoni campaign. The term "Hail Mary pass" came up in most pundits' predictions of the Gorgoni strategy.

The Gorgonis were comfortably ensconced in a spacious two story modern villa with a balcony that looked out upon a banyan tree of immense girth, one branch close enough to touch, and beyond it a heated swimming pool and sauna, and beyond that the green of the ninth hole. Delighted to have the day off the campaign trail to relax, Gorgoni arose at seven a.m., threw on jeans and a cotton shirt, and went straight to the balcony to relax on a chaise lounge and read *The Lost Steps* by Alejo Carpentier, the novel he had promised himself he would finish before election day. He read very slowly, his mind occupied with the contrast between his own peculiar fate, navigating his way through a media-dominated political culture that often seemed as silly as it was sterile, and the fate of Carpentier, his years in Paris in the thirties, navigating his way through the political culture of his day, hanging out with the likes of Picasso and Neruda. Surely Carpentier lived the richer life, he thought. Surely there was something to be said for a life of the mind, a life of letters, and a time when culture was still something to be hewn out of the rock of human experience. Could the world ever rewind to the purer excitement of a simpler time? What could a politician, even a president, do to reinvent that? He supposed that monks could still find simplicity and a life of the mind, but only by cloistering themselves, shutting themselves off from the world. How could one engage the world and yet not be cheapened by the aggressive dumbing-down that was the lifeblood of the commercial culture, the festering underbelly of the polity he sought to lead? His thoughts were interrupted by the ringtone of his cell phone, and he envied Carpentier's luck in never encountering one. Surely *The Lost Steps* couldn't have been written if its author couldn't find a way to be out of reach.

"Hello?"

"What are you doing, answering your phone? You should be preparing for the debate."

"How's the weather in Louisiana?"

"Beautiful day for greyhounds. They like it humid, and today it's stickier than old gum in glue. What are you doing to prepare?"

"I'm engaging my mind."

"*Oy vey.*"

191

"I was thinking, I'd like to be the first president to go to Havana."

"Okay, truly a lovely thought, but don't announce it before the election. You can't win without Florida."

"What are we afraid of? I think I can make their little experiment with Communism look as sad and backward as it is."

"Promise me, not a word of this in the debate."

"I mean, all they have to do is pick me up at the Havana airport in a fifty-six Chevy, and I think their little sixty-year experiment will be over."

"Alvin tells me you're still refusing to do mock debates."

"Yeah, I'd hate to win one of those and get overconfident."

"But you're going to prepare, right?"

"Either I'm delusional, Monty, or we got 'em where we want 'em."

"Yeah, I'd say it's definitely one or the other. Just make the son of a bitch explode. It would be real sweet if we could get a flash of temper. So what exactly are you doing to prepare?"

"I'll stay up late and do whatever I need to do. Have a little faith in me."

His legs had a tendency to sink; it was only by force of will that he could keep them elevated and kicking. He had the unpleasant sensation of chlorine invading all his facial cavities, and time and again had been reduced to spitting as the preferable alternative to swallowing. But Caroline had helped him patiently, holding him aloft at the stomach and allowing him to work on his stroke and his kick, and after that exercise he had managed to swim across the pool and back, although he knew his form was lacking. The water was warm, heated if anything too much, and the moon was full, lighting up the night. He found it liberating that only he and Caroline were in the pool. Even the Secret Service contingent had graciously stepped back and given them some privacy. Although swimming was more pleasant now that he was successfully managing, as he never had before, to keep his body afloat, he climbed out of the pool behind Caroline with a sense of relief. They both grabbed towels that rested on a colorful Mexican-tiled low wall separating the pool area from the villa.

"I can do this," Gorgoni said. "I made some real headway."

"Not too bad," Caroline said, "for a beginner."

"I still have to work on my kick," Gorgoni said. He looked up at the high diving board, intrigued. He wondered what it would be like to bounce up and down on that plank in preparation for a disciplined flight into the water.

Caroline caught his gaze. "Don't even *think* about it," she said. "I just hope you're ready for the debate."

"Oh, almost forgot about that. Piece of cake. I think my stroke is coming along."

He hopped on his left leg and banged the heel of his right hand against his right ear to try to get the water out. Caroline looked at him with concern, though he knew it had nothing to do with the water in his ear.

Caroline chose for her husband a blue-grey suit with a white shirt and mauve tie, and she fastened an American flag pin on his lapel. "Just in case someone doesn't know what country you're from," she said, as she often did when she pinned it on. "You look dashing. Are you going to have your usual pre-debate snack?"

"Banana and dry toast," he said.

"Why don't you at least put jam on the toast?"

"I'm better on-air after dry toast. I had jam on my toast before the yuan devaluation debacle on *Face the Nation*. Never again."

"Maybe it was the wrong kind of jam."

"Don't be ridiculous. It was the fact of jam."

"Okay. Don't get any banana on your mustache."

After that early afternoon snack, they were driven to the campus of the University of Tampa, and pulled up in front of the McKay Auditorium, where the debate would take place. Hours of stage preparation and sound checks followed. Kalani requested that the height of Gorgoni's podium be raised two inches, and the adjustment was made. The lighting and sound were approved by both sides. Gorgoni was relaxing with Caroline in the green room, about ninety minutes before the debate would start, when there was a knock on the door; his security detail ushered in none other than Governor Malcolm Benneton, in a dark blue suit, set off by a pale yellow shirt and a purple tie, with the folded corners of a red handkerchief popping out of his jacket pocket.

"Evan, just wanted to say hello, and wish you well, though not too well," Benneton said, with a smile. "Hello, Caroline," he added with a wave.

Gorgoni and Caroline sprung up to shake Benneton's hand.

"Let's see if we can still speak to the issues that matter," Gorgoni said.

"That's my intention," Benneton said. "Although we sometimes disagree about what matters."

"You look very sharp, Governor," Caroline said.

"Yes. If they judge us on appearance, I'm a distinct underdog," Gorgoni said.

"Well, according to the polls, you've got that honor anyway."

"Don't be fooled by the polls. That's my rope-a-dope strategy."

Benneton laughed. "By all means, keep it going. Let's have a good show tonight."

"See you later," Gorgoni said, as Benneton walked out.

Gorgoni popped his head out the door to watch Benneton walk down the hall, his head buried in a black briefing book handed to him by one of his aides. Then Gorgoni turned back into the green room, hopped on his left leg, and banged his right hand against his right ear, which still felt like it had water in it.

George Stephanopoulos, the moderator, welcomed the Tampa audience and the national audience graciously, and then introduced the two candidates, who walked onto the stage simultaneously to a handsome round of applause. They met in the middle of the stage, in between their respective podiums, and shook hands.

"Evan, nice to see you again," Benneton said with a broad smile, clearly feeling obligated to say something during the handshake.

"Good to see you, Governor Mudge," Gorgoni said. "Oh, did I say Mudge? I'm sorry, I confused you with someone else."

Benneton froze at hearing those words, and his look hardened. He took his first step to his podium backwards, then turned around and hurried to his place, gripping his podium like a drowning man might grip a rock.

"Governor, by coin toss, the first question goes to you," George Stephanopoulos said. "A climate change bill limiting carbon emissions passed the Senate but is currently dead in the

House. If it were to pass both chambers, would you sign it as president?"

Benneton had the air of a man who did not know where he was. He stood there mutely for a moment, then said, "Uh...I'm sorry, could you repeat the question?"

"Would you sign the climate change bill in its current form?" George Stephanopoulus asked.

"No, never, and you can take that to the bank. That's a Democratic piece of legislation founded on a belief that government can solve all our problems," Benneton said. "It's a classic case of big government getting in the way of free enterprise. If we pass the climate change bill, we'll lose hundreds of thousands of jobs. Those are real jobs, while climate change is only a theory, and a discredited theory at that."

"Congressman, do you believe climate change is a discredited theory?" George Stephanopoulos asked.

"No, and neither does he," Gorgoni said.

Benneton wore an expression of disbelief.

"Are you calling me a liar?" he asked.

"It gets hotter every year all over the planet," Gorgoni said.

"That could be a natural cycle—"

"Wildfires across America, across Russia, across Australia, fish washing up dead on the beaches of the Atlantic because the water's too hot."

"There were blizzards last winter—the worst in ages!"

"As predicted. As the top of the world heats up, artic air moves down and disrupts our natural warming currents—you know that very well."

"I do not—don't tell me what I know!" Benneton exploded, evidently flustered. "And you're going to overcome the so-called warming with zero population growth?"

"It's our only hope," Gorgoni said.

"If we stop growing our population, it'll destroy the economy! It's un-American, unworkable, and it offends every bone in my body!"

George Stephanopoulos' eyes lit up. The debate was going on without his help.

"We have over three hundred million Americans," Gorgoni said. "Our population has more than doubled in our lifetimes. When your grandchildren are fifty or sixty, are there going to be six hundred million?"

"Why not?"

"Where the heck are you going to put the next three hundred million? How will you fit their cars on the roads? Where's the energy going to come from? And the food? How will you keep the pollution from choking them? We've already reached the limit."

"You're underestimating American ingenuity!"

"Are you okay with a billion Americans? Two billion? There are no limits?"

"Of course there are limits."

"So what's the limit?"

"I don't know. Maybe six hundred million. We've got a long way to go. Plenty of open spaces—"

"But we stop at six hundred million? We stop on a dime at that time?"

"Yes. We could."

"I thought that would destroy the economy?"

"I'm not worried about the economy sixty years from now!"

"No, clearly you're not worried about anything except saying whatever you need to say to get elected."

Benneton looked apoplectic. He had the rage of a man who apparently felt that he had been tricked somehow.

"See? Another personal attack! That's what this campaign is really about—character!"

"Governor, exactly what kind of personal attacks do you feel the congressman has made against you?" George Stephanopoulos asked.

Benneton paused and scratched his ear. "Well, he knows very well."

"But surely you must be referring to some specific personal attack—"

"Well, there have been threats," Benneton said.

"What kind of threats?" George Stephanopoulos asked, with seemingly genuine interest.

"Look, America has to trust the person in the Oval Office. And my opponent has been hiding from the American people everything about his life, his family, his wife's marriages, right down to the food they eat. The man wants zero population growth and he himself is a cipher!"

George Stephanopoulos turned to Gorgoni.

"Congressman, is this election all about character, and have you been hiding anything about yours?"

"George, we are all pop-ups on the earth. And in this all-too-brief period during which we pop up, why waste a minute attacking one another or responding to unfounded attacks? During my own very insignificant pop-up, my time on Earth, it will matter very little whether I ever occupy the White House. But during the pop-ups of three hundred million plus Americans, it will matter very much whether we protect our land, our seas, our climate, or whether we devote ourselves to maximizing greed by relentlessly burning the carbon that has been happily sequestered within the earth for millions of years. What is an election but an expression of the very point and purpose of popping up? If you want to love and cherish and sustain the precious gift of the earth onto which we have all had the good fortune to pop up, I ask for your vote."

While the eccentricity of Gorgoni's reference to "pop-ups on the earth" drew howls from Fox News, the media reaction to the debate was fairly uniform: Gorgoni had seemed poised and likeable; Benneton had appeared out-of-sorts and had committed any number of *non sequiturs*. It was by all accounts, including instant polling, a win for Gorgoni, but whether it was a big enough win to overcome Benneton's substantial lead was a subject of debate. On MSNBC, Chris Matthews and Lawrence O'Donnell appeared exuberant.

"Lawrence, I thought it was a knockout," Chris Matthews said. "Benneton looked dazed and confused from the beginning, while Gorgoni was composed, crisp, and rational."

"Chris, from the moment that Benneton claimed that Gorgoni had made personal attacks against him but could not name a single such attack, he was toast."

"Absolutely. I agree completely. And toast is of course the apt metaphor because it pops up."

Melanie's overnight polling showed Benneton's lead cut in half, and was cause for optimism in the Gorgoni camp. But the media had already moved on to something else that could potentially dwarf the impact of the debate: a *New York Times* front page story charging that Malcolm Benneton had a narcolepsy problem that he appeared to be hiding from the public. Gorgoni saw the story on the morning news at six a.m., read it online, and immediately went out on the balcony overlooking the banyan and phoned Monty.

Monty answered the phone with the dazed "hello" of a man awakened from a deep sleep.

"*The New York Times* is reporting that Benneton is a narcoleptic," Gorgoni said.

"Is that right?" Monty said.

"I wonder who their source was."

"Whoever it was should be considered a national hero, in my opinion. Can't wait to read the article—let me go to the computer."

"Monty, I told you we didn't need to do this."

"Actually, what you told us before the last debate was that you were going to do it yourself, which you proceeded not to do."

"I won the debate."

"Yes, you did—good for three or four points. You were down eight."

"I gave you and the staff a direct order not to leak anything."

"I can't believe I have to remind you of this, but I don't work for your campaign. I'm just a patriotic citizen."

Gorgoni sighed deeply.

"This is my campaign! I have the right to win the way I want to!"

"Wrong on both counts! It's not *your* campaign! What about the five million plus people who have sent in contributions? Don't you owe them something, like at least, I don't know, maybe trying to win?"

"I'm trying to win."

"You may think you are, but you don't get to repeal all the laws of politics! You've already repealed a lot of them, I'll give you credit for that, but you don't get to repeal them all! You don't get to decide that the American people shouldn't know that the other would-be president can't stay awake! You don't get to decide that! If no one else will, then I'll resolve that issue, and I'll weigh national security on one hand, and on the other hand, I'll weigh your delicate feelings about not wanting to appear too critical. And I'll make the appropriate decision as a patriot."

"I wish I could fire you again."

"I'm not even getting paid, and I'm winning you the election. Don't be an ingrate."

Gorgoni reached out and laid his hand on a solid, smooth arm of the banyan. He let out an anguished moan.

"So what's next?" he asked.

"What's next? Next is enjoying the momentum for the final two weeks of the campaign! Next is the narcolepsy story drowning out every other message they want to get out while their campaign implodes and operatives quit. Next is Republicans calling for Benneton's head for hiding this from them. Next is a political earthquake, my friend. Hey, I got a great idea, let me call Alvin."

"What's the idea?"

"You should wrap up the campaign right where you are, in Tampa, to bring back the memories of your final triumphant debate. You with me?"

"Fine with me. I like it here."

"Plus Florida will clinch it for you."

"I like the humidity."

"Feeling better?"

"I guess."

"You know, when you're president, people are going to do end-runs around you all the time, so get used to it."

"Yeah, I suppose."

"Okay. Now relax, Evan. Enjoy the ride."

Gorgoni nodded. He began to feel that there was, after all, something karmic and appropriate about the *New York Times* story.

"Hey, I got some good news."

"What?"

"I can swim."

"*Mazel tov.*"

The final two weeks of the campaign were a glorious blur, the news cycle every day overwhelmed by new revelations in the narcolepsy story, and by Benneton's evolving explanations, which became the subject of late-night comedy, while Gorgoni crisscrossed the country, generating excitement wherever he went. Everything was suddenly getting much easier. Hannah Svoboda joked that she no longer had to advance events; she could just Tweet a reference to the next event and it would advance itself. Kalani felt no further pressure to spin anything. Caroline suddenly found herself able to sleep deeply in hotel rooms. And Gorgoni took pleasure in the fact that he had managed to run an entire campaign without a single prepared or written speech; his reward for that, he told himself, was an avalanche of luck.

Before he knew it he found himself right back where he had learned to swim, in the deluxe golf villa outside of Tampa, overlooking the ninth hole, having closed out the campaign earlier that afternoon with an Election Day rally at the University of South Florida Sun Dome, which was packed to the rafters with a young and wildly enthusiastic crowd.

At five, the team gathered in their villa to await the returns: Alvin, Kalani, Melanie, Hannah, Jake and his wife Jolene and their two sons, and of course the whole Gorgoni family. The plan was to await the judgment of the people; have the obligatory well-wishing, brief phone conversation with Benneton; then proceed to a rally in downtown Tampa where Gorgoni would either declare victory or make his concession. Tethered to a host of wireless devices, Melanie was upbeat that the former scenario was more likely; internal exit polls from across the country were looking good, she said, announcing each such piece of evidence as it came in.

Moments before the early returns could be reported by the broadcast networks, there was a knock on the door. Alvin said, "I wonder who that could be?" with the air of a man confident of the answer. He opened the door, letting in a very jaunty Monty Berg, in white slacks and a blue blazer, looking like a yacht owner.

"I was in the neighborhood," Monty said.

"Monty, I didn't know you were a golfer," Jake said.

"I never was, but I'm going to take it up as soon as the new president passes his bill requiring fat people to play sports."

"You weren't listening clearly," Gorgoni said, giving Monty a bear hug. "I said fit people."

"Oh, much better," Monty said. "Now nothing will change for me at all. That's what I look for in a president."

The returns first came in from the East Coast, with Gorgoni comfortably carrying all of New England and the Mid-Atlantic States. Virginia and North Carolina were close, but with two thirds of the votes counted they had begun to swing Gorgoni's way as the urban vote came in, and the networks called them for Gorgoni with about three-quarters of the votes in. Florida went blue as well, by a safe margin, called by the networks one after the other with only twenty percent of the votes counted, as cheers erupted around the room. Benneton was left carrying only South Carolina and Georgia along the Atlantic Coast.

The electoral votes began to pile up in the blue column as the returns moved further west, and within a couple of hours, after Ohio had been added the blue column along with Michigan and Wisconsin, there was not much suspense left.

Monty sat closest to the TV screen, gorging on peanuts without ever looking at the bowl that he was so efficiently emptying.

"These are way too salty," he said. "First thing you should do by executive order is cut the salt in half on roasted peanuts."

"Not exactly my top priority," Gorgoni said.

"Okay, Mr. Bigshot, what's your top priority?"

"I still want to get those damned stickers off fruit."

"You're making a classic political error. More people eat salted peanuts."

"A president leads by example."

"That doesn't apply to fruit."

"Hey, Dad, can we get a vegan White House chef?" Nicole asked.

"Yes, we can," Gorgoni said.

"I don't imagine you have a victory speech written?" Monty said.

"Are you putting me on?" Gorgoni said.

A map of Illinois appeared onto the screen.

"Shhh! Here it comes," Kalani said.

Illinois turned blue; Gorgoni's picture appeared next to it with a checkmark, and the words "20 Electoral Votes."

"Hold everything. Hold everything," Brian Williams was saying in his election night studio. "We now project that Illinois will go to Evan Nathan Gorgoni, and with it the presidency of the United States of America."

Pandemonium broke out in the villa overlooking the ninth hole. Gorgoni and Caroline kissed the way Al Gore and Tipper once had, oblivious to the scene around them. Monty threw a big handful of peanuts into the air. Wisdom barked and went after all the strewn nuts. The young people were shouting and jumping up and down and then grabbing their cell phones to snap selfies and to send texts and Tweets. Tears came to Kalani's eyes. Alvin shook everyone's hand one-by-one, expressed his gratitude, and then pulled each handshake into an embrace. Gorgoni and Caroline gave heartfelt hugs and kisses to everyone in the room.

And then, as the group's attention began to turn back to the TV screen, to see and hear what the wider world was saying about their victory, Gorgoni slipped out of the living room suite and into the bedroom. He threw his jacket on the bed, opened the sliding glass balcony door, and stepped out onto the balcony for some air, sliding the glass door behind him. It was an unusually balmy November night, with a faint scent of lemon in the air. The pool area was dimly illuminated by copper-domed path lights and by the light of an oblong moon. The quiet was astonishing. Far in the distance he saw a discrete white flash of fireworks in the sky.

A thick branch of the banyan brushed against the waist-high railing before elbowing and rising higher and away from the building. Other branches of the banyan ran only a few feet below this one. Gorgoni sat atop the railing and, holding onto the thick branch, maneuvered his legs over the railing so that his back was to the villa and he was facing the pool. He clasped his hands firmly around the branch and let himself slide off the railing, suspending himself in the air until his feet found a lower branch of the banyan, and then he reached to the side to find another, thinner branch from which to suspend himself. One more step down onto still another, lower branch, and from there he was able to jump a mere two feet onto the grass, where he landed upright.

At first he worried that he had sprained an ankle but with each step he felt stronger as he walked towards the pool. He took off his shoes and socks first, then stripped off his shirt and then his pants, dropping them on a chaise lounge. He was wearing nothing but his briefs and his wedding ring. He took off the wedding ring and put it carefully in one of the shoes. He walked towards the high diving board. Without hesitation, he began climbing the ten rungs to the top, leaning back a little as he climbed, feeling the tension in his arms.

Once atop the board, he walked tentatively towards its forward edge, and looked down to the pool. With his arms at his side, he tried jumping an inch or two into the air to get a sense of the board's bounce. He turned and walked back toward the base of the board. Then he turned forward again and concentrated on the distance in front of him—the length of the board. He started to run forward, did a little skip, then jumped to the tip of the board, bounced straight up into the air, landed back down on the board, and now bounced forward with his hands clasped above his head, his dive taking him on an upward trajectory for a brief moment before he headed down towards the water.

His form was far from perfect, but for the first dive of a middle-aged man, it wasn't half-bad.

Recipes

(p.5) "Hey, should I cook tonight?" Gorgoni said.
"How about I make my classic shiitake stew?"

RED LENTIL SHIITAKE STEW
(SERVES 4)

1 CUP DRY RED LENTILS

2¼ CUPS WATER

4 MEDIUM FRESH SHIITAKE
   MUSHROOMS, SLICED

1 DRY BAY LEAF

½ CUP THINLY CHOPPED RED ONION

½ TEASPOON GINGER POWDER

¾ TEASPOON CORIANDER

½ TEASPOON CUMIN

2 TABLESPOONS CHOPPED FRESH
   PARSLEY FOR GARNISH

1 TABLESPOON SCALLIONS FOR
   GARNISH

SEA SALT, TO TASTE

WHITE PEPPER, TO TASTE

Rinse the red lentils, and soak for at least 20-30 minutes. Discard the soaking water.

In a pot, combine the red lentils with the water and bring to a boil, then simmer for 20 minutes. Add sliced shiitake mushrooms and onion, the bay leaf, ginger powder, coriander, and cumin, and continue simmering for 20 more minutes. In the last minute of simmering, add the sea salt and white pepper and stir in chopped scallions and chopped parsley. Serve with brown rice or mashed potatoes.

(p.18) *"I'll bet it's going to be weird when you go back to Washington now," Nicole said, serving herself some mashed Japanese sweet potatoes.*

MASHED JAPANESE SWEET POTATOES

(SERVES 2-3 AS A SIDE DISH)

2 STEAMED PEELED JAPANESE SWEET POTATOES

6 CARDAMOM PODS

½ TEASPOON TURMERIC (OPTIONAL)

2 TABLESPOONS FRESH LEMON JUICE

½ CUP UNSWEETENED SOY MILK OR UNSWEETENED ALMOND MILK

1 TABLESPOON GARLIC POWDER

4 ROASTED GARLIC CLOVES, CHOPPED INTO SMALL PIECES

4 TABLESPOONS FINELY CHOPPED SCALLIONS

COCONUT AMINOS, TO TASTE

SEA SALT, TO TASTE

Steam the sweet potatoes until soft. Grind the seeds from the cardamom pods into a powder in a mortar. Then add all the ingredients to the still-hot steamed sweet potatoes and mash evenly.

(p.18) *"Let me go with you for a week,"*
Caroline said, sipping her miso soup.

BARLEY MISO SOUP
(SERVES 4)

¼ CUP DRY BARLEY

6 CUPS PLUS 5 TABLESPOONS OF
   WATER

1 CELERY STALK, THINLY SLICED

1 CARROT, SLICED

2 ONIONS, PEELED AND DICED

½ CUP SLICED BUTTON MUSHROOMS

3 TABLESPOONS WHITE MISO

2 TABLESPOONS CHOPPED PARSLEY

PINCH OF SEA SALT

TOASTED NORI FOR GARNISH
   (OPTIONAL)

Soak the barley overnight. Discard the soaking water, rinse the barley, and put in a pot with 6 cups of water and pinch of sea salt. Simmer covered until barley is tender, for about 1 hour. Add remaining ingredients except for the parsley. Bring the soup almost to a boil, then lower the flame and simmer, covered, until the vegetables are tender (about 15 minutes).

Prepare the miso: mix the miso paste in a cup with 5 tablespoons of water, then gradually add into it 6-8 tablespoons of the liquid from the soup, and stir well. Remove the soup from the heat and add the miso to it. Bring the soup almost to a boil, lower the flame and simmer for 2-3 minutes. Stir in parsley. Garnish with toasted nori if desired. Serve.

(p.18) *"Why?" Gorgoni said, examining vegetables he did not recognize on his macrobiotic plate.*

MACROBIOTIC PLATE
(SERVES 4)

1 CUP DRY MILLET

1 DRY PIECE OF KOMBU (POSTAGE
STAMP SIZE)

¼ CUP CHOPPED ONIONS

½ CUP BUTTERNUT OR KABOCHA
SQUASH, CUT INTO SMALL CUBES

¼ CUP DAIKON ROOT, CUT INTO
MATCH STICKS

¼ CUP CELERY ROOT (CELERIAC),
CUT INTO SMALL CUBES

¼ CUP CHOPPED CARROT

FRESH BURDOCK ROOT (ABOUT 2
INCHES), PEELED AND FINELY
SLICED

2½ CUPS WATER (FOR COOKING,
NOT FOR SOAKING)

SEA SALT, TO TASTE

CHOPPED SCALLIONS FOR GARNISH

Rinse the millet, then soak in water overnight together with the kombu. Discard the soaking water, and layer the millet and kombu on the bottom of the pot with the vegetables on top of the millet. Add 2½ cups of water. Bring almost to a boil, then lower the flame to a simmer, sprinkle the sea salt, and cover the pot. Simmer for 40-50 minutes on a flame deflector to prevent burning. Remove from the stove and let sit covered for a few minutes before serving. Drizzle with miso tahini dressing (next recipe), and garnish with scallions.

MISO TAHINI DRESSING
(SERVES 4)

3 TABLESPOONS TAHINI

1½ TEASPOONS SWEET WHITE MISO

⅓ CUP WATER

2 TABLESPOONS FRESHLY
SQUEEZED LEMON JUICE

1 TABLESPOON FRESH CHOPPED PARSLEY

Using a spoon, mix the tahini with the miso in a small cup. Start slowly adding the water and keep mixing to create the consistency of a smooth paste. Mix with the remaining water to get a liquidy consistency, then add the lemon juice and mix again. (The lemon juice will thicken the mixture a little bit.) If the consistency is too thick, a little more water can be added. Add the chopped parsley, stir, transfer to a small sauce pot, and simmer gently 5-10 minutes (preferably over a flame deflector) while stirring occasionally. Do not allow to boil.

(p.27) *They walked to* Paros, *a Greek place where, over plates of braised dandelion, roasted potatoes, tzatziki, hummus, baba ganoush, and spiced olives, they waxed collectively nostalgic over their early years in politics.*

TZATZIKI

(SERVES 6 AS APPETIZER)

1 MEDIUM-TO-LARGE CUCUMBER

16 OZ. PLAIN NON-DAIRY YOGURT

   (UNSWEETENED IF POSSIBLE)

1 CLOVE RAW GARLIC, MINCED

1 TABLESPOON LEMON JUICE

1 TABLESPOON CHOPPED FRESH DILL

SEA SALT, TO TASTE

FRESHLY GROUND BLACK PEPPER,

   TO TASTE

Peel the cucumber, discard seeds, grate the cucumber, and strain the liquid. Combine the grated cucumber with all other ingredients (except sea salt and pepper) in food processor, pulse, then season with sea salt and pepper, and chill for at least an hour before serving.

ROASTED GARLIC ARTICHOKE HUMMUS
(SERVES 6 AS APPETIZER)

14-15 OZ. CAN GARBANZO BEANS, DRAINED AND RINSED

8-10 OZ. MARINATED ARTICHOKE HEARTS

3 TABLESPOONS CHOPPED SCALLIONS

3 TABLESPOONS TAHINI

1 GARLIC HEAD, ROASTED

2 TABLESPOONS LEMON JUICE

SEA SALT AND PEPPER, TO TASTE

To roast the garlic: peel each clove and put into oven pre-heated at 350 degrees for about 5 minutes or until lightly golden.

Place all ingredients in food processor. Blend to a creamy consistency.

BABA GANOUSH

(SERVES 4-6 AS APPETIZER)

1 MEDIUM-SIZED EGGPLANT

¼ CUP CHOPPED SCALLIONS

2 TABLESPOONS TAHINI

2 TABLESPOONS FRESH LEMON JUICE

SEA SALT AND PEPPER, TO TASTE

Wrap eggplant in aluminum foil and bake at 400 degrees for 60 minutes (or until soft). Remove from the foil and pull the skin off the eggplant while it is still hot. Scoop out eggplant seeds and discard. Mash the peeled eggplant and chopped scallions together using a fork or wooden spoon. Add the tahini and lemon juice and mix well. Season to taste with sea salt and pepper.

(p.32) She always brought a sandwich from home, usually homemade sunflower pâté with alfalfa sprouts on rye, and she sat with a new group of friends...

SUNFLOWER PÂTÉ

(SERVES 10 AS APPETIZER)

1 MEDIUM-TO-LARGE RAW YELLOW-SKIN POTATO, PEELED AND CHOPPED

1 CUP RAW SUNFLOWER SEEDS

¼ CUP FLAX SEEDS

½ CUP BROWN RICE FLOUR

1 MEDIUM ONION, CHOPPED

1 CELERY STALK, CHOPPED

1 CARROT, CHOPPED

½ CUP NUTRITIONAL YEAST

3 TABLESPOONS ITALIAN SEASONINGS

1 CUP COLD WATER

¾ TEASPOON SEA SALT

¼ TEASPOON GROUND WHITE PEPPER

In the food processor, chop the sunflower seeds coarsely. Add the remaining ingredients and process into a smooth consistency. Pre-heat oven to 350 degrees. Line a loaf pan with parchment paper (to avoid use of oil). Pour in the mixture and bake uncovered for 1 hour or until golden brown. Let cool to thicken before cutting into slices and serving.

(p.33) Caroline sat on the wood-framed, brown tweed couch in the cozy Gorgoni den, a plate of date confections before her on the beaten-up walnut coffee table, and watched The Situation Room on CNN.

CHOCOLATE DATE NUT BALLS
(SERVES 6)

10 PITTED MOIST DATES

²/₃ CUP ALMONDS

4 TABLESPOONS FRESHLY SQUEEZED
   ORANGE JUICE

1 TABLESPOON FRESH LEMON JUICE

¼ TEASPOON ORANGE FLAVOR OR
   EXTRACT

½ TEASPOON FRESH LEMON ZEST

4 TABLESPOONS COCOA POWDER,
   PLUS EXTRA COCOA POWDER FOR
   DUSTING THE BALLS

If the dates are too dry, they should be soaked in water or coconut water for half an hour. Crush the almonds into small pieces in a food processor. Chop the dates with a knife into tiny pieces. Combine all the ingredients in a bowl and mix them thoroughly by hand. Form into balls. (The recipe will yield 12 balls.) Then roll the balls in the remaining cocoa powder to create an even coating. Cool in the fridge for a few hours before serving.

(p.44) Caroline stopped herself in the midst of serving cucumber soup for Nicole, Mandy, and herself.

CHILLED CUCUMBER SOUP
(SERVES 2)

2 LARGE CUCUMBERS

1 AVOCADO

1 LARGE GARLIC CLOVE

¼ CUP DENSELY PACKED FRESH
MINT OR BASIL

3 TABLESPOONS CHOPPED ONION

3 TABLESPOONS LEMON JUICE

SEA SALT, TO TASTE

Peel the cucumbers and cut into chunks after scooping out any seeds. In a blender, combine all ingredients. Blend until smooth. Chill before serving for at least one hour.

Note: this can also double as a dressing. For the dressing, be sure to use the basil instead of mint.

(p.55) *Caroline whipped up a dinner of corkscrew artichoke pasta with basil pesto, long a favorite of Gorgoni's, to celebrate his unexpected presence.*

BASIL PESTO
(SERVES 4)

½ CUP DENSELY PACKED FRESH
   PARSLEY LEAVES
1 CUP DENSELY PACKED FRESH BASIL
   LEAVES

¼ CUP WALNUTS, COARSELY CHOPPED
3 CLOVES LIGHTLY ROASTED
   GARLIC, CHOPPED
SEA SALT AND PEPPER, TO TASTE

Place the basil and parsley on the bottom of the food processor, and on top of them place the chopped garlic and walnuts. Add sea salt and pepper. Blend all the ingredients to a loose consistency. Do not over-process to a mushy consistency.

(p.60) *"I'm running for president, Mom," Gorgoni said. They were sitting in the facility's dining room, each table appointed with a bouquet of tulips, and had just been served a vegetable casserole.*

VEGETABLE CASSEROLE
(SERVES 4)

FOR THE CASSEROLE BATTER (WHEAT OR GLUTEN-FREE):

$2/3$ CUP WHOLE WHEAT FLOUR OR BROWN RICE FLOUR

$2/3$ CUP PLUS 2 TABLESPOONS UNSWEETENED ALMOND MILK

2 HEAPING TABLESPOONS UNSWEETENED APPLE SAUCE

$1\frac{1}{4}$ TEASPOON BAKING POWDER

2 TEASPOONS DRIED MARJORAM

$\frac{1}{2}$ TEASPOON GARLIC POWDER

PINCH OF SEA SALT

FOR THE FILLING:

1 SMALL-TO-MEDIUM YAM, SLICED

1 SMALL-TO-MEDIUM JAPANESE SWEET POTATO, SLICED

2 CUPS FRESH SLICED BUTTON MUSHROOMS (NO STEMS)

$\frac{1}{2}$ CUP COARSELY CHOPPED BASIL

$2/3$ CUP FROZEN GREEN PEAS

$\frac{1}{2}$ MEDIUM ONION, CHOPPED THINLY

1 SPRIG FRESH ROSEMARY

1 TABLESPOON CHOPPED FRESH SAGE

$\frac{1}{2}$ CUP OF WATER

$1\frac{1}{2}$ TABLESPOON RAW COCONUT AMINOS (OPTIONAL)

SEA SALT, TO TASTE

WHITE PEPPER, TO TASTE (OPTIONAL)

Let the green peas thaw. Steam the sweet potato and yam until soft, then let cool. Cook the mushrooms and onions in ½ cup of water in a sauce pan for about 15-20 minutes; in the last few minutes of cooking add fresh sage. In the last minute of cooking, add sea salt and pepper to taste. You should still have some liquid in the sauce pan that is now an aromatic sauce.

To make the batter: combine all the dry ingredients (flour, baking powder, marjoram, garlic powder, sea salt) and mix well in a bowl. Combine the wet ingredients (almond milk and apple sauce) in a cup. Add the wet mixture to the dry mixture and gently stir to a smooth consistency.

In the casserole dish, begin to create the first layer of the casserole with slices of the steamed Japanese sweet potato. Fill up the empty spaces between the slices with the thawed green peas. Fill in the spaces around the wall of the casserole dish with pieces of fresh rosemary. On the top of the completed first layer, spread a layer of the cooked mushrooms and onions with its liquid. Begin creating the third (and last) layer with slices of the steamed yams. Drizzle over the yams the raw coconut aminos (if using), and scatter the chopped basil. Spread the batter over the top. The spaces between the yam slices will be filled in by the batter.

Pre-heat oven to 350 degrees. Bake uncovered for 40-50 minutes. Take out of the oven and let stand, covered, for 15 minutes before serving. (The dough doesn't have any oil and to retain moisture it needs to be covered while still hot.) For the gluten-free version, allow to bake for 5-10 extra minutes.

(p.64) *"This is delicious," Monty said. "I never had cheese like this."*
"Probably not," Caroline said.

MILD HERB ALMOND CHEESE
(SERVES 4)

1 CUP ALMONDS, SOAKED IN WATER FOR 6-8 HOURS

¼ CUP + 4 TABLESPOONS COCONUT WATER

2 TEASPOONS MILD WHITE MISO

1 TABLESPOON FRESH MARJORAM

1 CLOVE RAW GARLIC

1 TABLESPOON CHOPPED RED ONION

1 TABLESPOON CHOPPED PARSLEY

½ TEASPOON FRESHLY SQUEEZED LEMON JUICE

SEA SALT, TO TASTE

Rinse the soaked almonds. Remove the skins. (After soaking, the skins peel easily.) Place the almonds in the food processor with the coconut water and chop until you obtain a smooth, light consistency. Then add the remaining ingredients to the food processor and process until thoroughly mixed. May be stored in the refrigerator for about three days.

(p.64) *"And these crackers are remarkably dry," Monty said. "It's my own recipe. Garlic flaxseed crackers. They're dehydrated."*

GARLIC HERB FLAXSEED CRACKERS
(SERVES 12)

2 CUPS FLAX SEEDS

4 TABLESPOONS APPLE SAUCE

3 CLOVES OF RAW GARLIC

$^2/_3$ CUP DENSELY PACKED FRESH
   BASIL LEAVES

$^1/_2$ CUP DENSELY PACKED FRESH
   PARSLEY LEAVES

12 PITTED SUNDRIED OLIVES

SEA SALT AND BLACK PEPPER,
   TO TASTE

Soak $1^1/_3$ cups of flax seeds in $^3/_4$ cup of water for 15 minutes until the water is absorbed. Chop the olives into small pieces. Combine in a food processor the soaked flax seeds with all the ingredients except the olives and dry flax seeds. Process for at least 5 minutes until the flax seeds are crushed. Add the olives for the final processing for 15-20 seconds. Place the mixture in a bowl together with the remaining $^2/_3$ cup dry flax seeds and mix well with a spoon.

Spread the mixture thinly onto dehydrator sheets. Dehydrate at 110 degrees for 4 hours. Then score the spread mixture into squares and continue dehydrating for an additional 8 hours or longer, depending on the desired crispiness. (Or instead of dehydrating, bake the crackers on parchment paper at 350 degrees for 45 minutes.)

(p.105) *"I'm happy for you," Monty said. "It's rare for borscht to play such a significant role in passion."*

RAW BEET BORSCHT
(SERVES 3-4)

1 MEDIUM-SIZED RED BEET

½ CUP OF RAW ALMONDS

½ CUP OF RAW SUNFLOWER SEEDS

3 CLOVES OF RAW GARLIC

½ TEASPOON CHOPPED GINGER

½ PEELED LEMON

½ PEELED LIME

1 CELERY STALK

2 SMALL CARROTS, PEELED

½ CUCUMBER

½ MEDIUM-SIZED ONION

½ MEDIUM-SIZED APPLE

½ AVOCADO

8 SPRIGS OF PARSLEY

5 SPRIGS OF CILANTRO

HANDFUL OF ALFALFA SPROUTS

2 TABLESPOONS RAW FLAX SEEDS

⅔ CUP OF WATER

BLACK PEPPER, TO TASTE

SEA SALT OR BRAGG'S LIQUID
AMINOS OR COCONUT AMINOS,
TO TASTE

Blend all ingredients in a power blender until smooth. Chill before serving.

(p.111) Caroline cooked one of the Gorgoni family's mainstay meals for dinner—a curry dish with a fruit cobbler for dessert—and the family ate in front of the television because CNN was running a special comparing the two all-but-official candidates who would square off in the fall.

MUNG BEAN CURRY
(SERVES 4-6)

3 CUPS OF WATER

1 CUP DRIED MUNG BEANS

2 DRY BAY LEAVES

½ MEDIUM ONION, CHOPPED

3 CLOVES RAW GARLIC, MINCED

1 TABLESPOON MINCED FRESH GINGER

½ TEASPOON TURMERIC POWDER

½ TEASPOON YELLOW CURRY

2 TABLESPOONS CHOPPED CILANTRO OR SWEET BASIL

1 TABLESPOON FRESHLY SQUEEZED LEMON JUICE

BLACK PEPPER, TO TASTE

SEA SALT OR BRAGG'S LIQUID AMINOS, TO TASTE

Rinse the mung beans, then soak overnight in water. The following day, discard the water, rinse the beans again, and add 3 cups of water and the bay leaves. Bring the beans almost to a boil, then reduce the flame to simmer. Pick up with a spoon the white foam that forms on the surface of the water and discard. Then simmer covered for about 40 minutes. Add the onions, garlic, ginger, turmeric, and curry, and continue simmering for an additional 20 minutes. When it's done, add pepper to taste, sea salt or Bragg's, lemon juice, chopped cilantro or basil, and stir. Serve over rice.

MIXED BERRY COBBLER
(SERVES 4)

½ CUP ALL-PURPOSE FLOUR (OR FOR GLUTEN-FREE VERSION, RICE FLOUR)

1 TABLESPOON ARROWROOT STARCH/FLOUR

1 TEASPOON BAKING POWDER

½ CUP ALMOND MILK (OR SOY MILK)

½ TEASPOON VANILLA EXTRACT

3 TABLESPOONS MAPLE SYRUP

1 TEASPOON ZEST OF FRESH LEMON

1½ CUP OF MIXED BERRIES (BLUEBERRIES, STRAWBERRIES, RASPBERRIES, BLACKBERRIES: FROZEN/THAWED, OR FRESH)

PINCH OF SEA SALT

1 TEASPOON COCONUT SUGAR

To create the batter: combine all-purpose flour, arrowroot starch, baking powder, and sea salt, and mix well in a bowl. In a measuring cup, mix and stir the almond milk, vanilla extract, maple syrup, and lemon zest. In the bowl with the dried ingredients, create a well in the middle. Pour the liquid mixture into the well. Stir gently until the consistency is smooth.

Preheat oven to 350 degrees. Put 1¼ cup of the berries in a small baking dish. Spoon the batter over the berries. Scatter the remaining ¼ cup of berries on top of the batter, and sprinkle with coconut sugar. Bake uncovered until lightly browned—about 40 minutes. Remove from oven and to retain moisture cover with a cotton cloth for at least 15 minutes before serving. Serve if desired with a scoop of non-dairy vanilla ice cream.

(p.135) *The run would build up for Gorgoni a hearty appetite
for his morning bowl of oatmeal with fruit and cinnamon;
the fruit was the only part of his ritual breakfast that would
change daily, though his favorite was organic blueberries.*

RAW STEEL-CUT OATS WITH BLUEBERRIES
(SERVES 2)

¾ CUP STEEL-CUT DRY OATS   2 DATES (PITTED)

¼ CUP WATER   CINNAMON (TO TASTE)

1 CUP BLUEBERRIES

Rinse the oats, and soak in water overnight. In the morning,
discard the soaking water, rinse the oats again, and combine
them in a power blender with ¼ cup of water, blueberries, and
dates, and blend until smooth. Serve with cinnamon sprinkled
on top.

RAW STEEL-CUT OATS WITH PERSIMMONS
(SERVES 2-3)

¾ CUP STEEL-CUT DRY OATS **1** DATE (PITTED)

¼ CUP WATER

3 FRESH DONUT-SHAPED FUJI
PERSIMMONS (PITTED)

Rinse the oats, and soak in water overnight. In the morning, discard the soaking water, rinse the oats again, and combine them in a power blender with ¼ cup of water, 3 persimmons, and one date. Blend until smooth.

Made in the USA
Lexington, KY
24 January 2015